Myriad Mirrors

Myriad Mirrors

Malayalam Women Writings

*Edited and Translated
by Sanju Ramachandran*

Srishti
PUBLISHERS & DISTRIBUTORS

SRISHTI PUBLISHERS & DISTRIBUTORS
64-A, Adhchini
Sri Aurobindo Marg
New Delhi 110 017
srishtipublishers@forindia.com
srishtipublishers@yahoo.com

ISBN 81-88575-04-6
Rs. 145.00

Cover design: Vinayak Bhattacharya

Typeset in AGaramond 11pt. by Skumar at Srishti

Printed and bound in India by
Saurabh Print-O-Pack, Noida

To Amma

Contents

Editor's Note

All cultures have their ways of telling stories. The short story is the strongest of all literary genres of Malayalam. Its form and substance have constantly evolved, the sculpting hands holding the chisel never wearing out, with at least one 'master' even denying the novel all together. The first Malayalam short story was written more than a century ago and since then it has become the most popular form of story telling.

In a state with the highest literacy rate and female to male ratio, women auto rickshaw drivers and petrol pump attendants are commonplace. Women hold high offices, lead protest marches in the scorching sun, sell tickets to travelers in transport buses. But, there are no women bar tenders or revelers in a land crazy after booze. No woman can be seen smoking in public anywhere in Kerala.

Predictably Malayalam women writers have a lot to say. The earliest among them, Lalithambika Antharjanam wrote about the cloistered life of Brahmin women and their woes at home, but was also sensitive to the societal caste inequities. A host of others followed giving voices to the old and new traumas in a world that gave liberty to learn, to step out of her house, but thwarted her individuality and attempts at spiritual realization. Her many revolts within and without the house were derided casually as, feminism, which obviously lost its meaning.

In Kerala, it is nobody's case that a man's world is wider than a woman's. But a woman is made to account for her characters and images at home, office or in the neighbourhood. There is still a search for one-to-one correlation in stories of unhappy marriages and sexual escapades with the woman author's life. The most promising of them all, Rajalakshmi committed suicide when she could not take it any longer. Antharjanam was put on the pedestal of Amma or mother and hence was spared all barbs and innuendoes. SaraswathiAmma chose to be single and not write for the last 16 years of her life. Madhavikutty or Kamala Suraiyya braved it all, in her writing as well as life. No wonder she became an icon for women aspiring to be themselves.

Most of the women writers featured in this anthology had or still have an independent career and, another full time job of a homemaker.

The term *pennezhuthu* (women's writing) does help to group together and promote writings by women. But many women writers feel they would be better off without any affirmative action. Kamala Suraiyya has once pointed this out in her inimitable style: "There are certain parts of the human body that differentiate a woman from a man. But a woman doesn't write with any of those." Of course, a woman's world is different, her sensibilities, priorities and perceptions are different. But then, every woman is different from another. As men do, women too respond to life's crises in separate ways, their experiences too are varied.

This anthology reflects the myriad ways in which women writers express themselves; these are the mirrors they hold to themselves and the world they live in. I have tried to make this book an assorted collection of stories, selecting those varied in style and substance. There are no underlying themes because they are meant to be different to capture the widest array of reflections possible – between Antharjanam and Sithara, these writers were born within a time scale of three quarters of a century.

Translating these stories has not been easy. Some of them are short and seemingly simple, but multi-layered. Some are splattered with local dialects that give them a distinct character. Getting all these nuances right in translation is next to impossible, is my only consolation.

Many friends and well-wishers have made my job easier. I owe this book to all the authors who have given their consent, the relatives of writers who hold the copyright, D.C Books, Kottayam, its manager G. Sreekumar, Abu Faizi, Sarita Varma and others who helped me obtain permission to compile these stories. I remember with special gratitude the efforts of Sarojini Kurup.

Women Writers of Malayalam edited by Dr. Sridevi K. Nair and *100 years 100 Stories* (both published by D.C. Books) have been ready reckoners.

My two little girls have put up with my long absences from

their midst and I thank Swapna for suffering their tantrums on my behalf. Rajasekhar Vundru, the dear friend, got the computer salvaged and hence the book. Thanks to, K. Sankaranarayanan, Manini Chatterjee, Manjippi and Ajaz Ashraf for their invaluable suggestions. Special thanks to cartoonist and Malayalam writer Bonny Thomas who happily volunteered to do the illustrations.

No words can express what I owe Rajesh, the driving force behind this book. I am grateful to Papa and Mamma, for being the indulgent parents they are, never interfering, never domineering. Thinking of it, everything goes back to them, reading, writing et al.

Above all I thank Amma, the most amazing human being I have ever met in my life. She is a person who sustained lives with her power of tolerance and strength of spirit. I thank her for the loads of couriers I received, for the innumerable phone calls she made, for her endearing words of encouragement and love, for her unfailing support all the time. I dedicate this book to her as a token of my gratitude for all that she has been to me these eleven years.

Sanju Ramachandran

Italo Calvino in Thrissur Express

Italo Calvino Thrissur Expressil

By Gita Hiranyan

The woman got in from a bus stop where dragonflies flew down to rest on electric lines. Ajay Maneri remembered that precisely. And there was a reason for this sharp recollection. He felt the flight of the dragonflies would make an ideal opening shot for his movie.

Now don't jump to conclude that Ajay Maneri is a movie director. For now, he is a mere would-be director. A flash back of his story runs like this.

Ajay Maneri – 39 years. No one would term him dark complexioned. He tried his best to hide his creeping baldness, combing up to the front some hair from just above the left ear. He stooped a bit, just the way those aware of their height would do, had a nonplussed expression and a face that was okay to look at. Did he spend his own money to drink? No, because there wasn't any.

It was stated earlier that he was a "would-be director." Let me explain. On certain evenings after a booze session with friend Sanal, he would sit in the empty Municipal Stadium and discuss the films he ought to direct. Some 12 years ago, Ajay had won a consolation prize in a screenplay competition held by Nana film magazine. The ghost of scriptwriting that possessed him then had since multiplied within, in the forms of song writing and direction.

He has other achievements too. The bug bites and the hot sun of big cities like Thiruvananthapuram, Ernakulam and Kozhikode that he suffered in the April-May months of film festivals and also the endless ennui of open forum debates.

He is sure of one thing. If John Abraham's[1] film production and distribution company Odessa were to be formed now, Ajay Maneri would be one of the founding members.

Anyway, he knew that one day he would be a TV – cinema magnate and had decided not to get married till then. Marriage was not his priority. He had a dream to pursue and that made him feel secure.

But that wasn't enough security for his mother to loan him pocket money. She was a hard nut to crack. He had to offer not just his but the whole world's self-respect at her lotus feet to haul a ten-rupee note out of her. But she wouldn't stop at that.

"The director still needs my pension money to buy a piece of loin cloth. You have grown as big as a buffalo. Can't you look around for a white-collar job that would earn you some

---

1 John Abraham, the maverick of Malayalam cinema is best known for his films *Amma Ariyan* and *Agraharathile Kazhuthai*

small change by the end of the month? Instead you fool around dreaming cinema," she would go on.

Loin-cloth! What a piece of dialogue! Just the bit for a perfect screenplay!

Whenever he heard it, Ajay would make a note: "Though she lived in a remote village mom was no character to be played out by Kaviyoor Ponnamma[2] – serene as a *thumpa* flower walking down the verandah on a moon-lit night with a lighted oil lamp in hand. Hers was a role that suited K.P.A.C Lalitha[3] better – a bit hot and sour and spicy."

But for his fantasies of movie making he wouldn't have survived these days of penury and humiliation. Sometimes he would think of actor Biju Menon. Then a 'humm' sound would rise from the bottom of his heart. That 'humm' could be translated this way: "We had staged several plays together for the Chempookavu temple festival and Viyyoor library anniversary. Now he has found his way into the royal courtyard of cinema, film magazines carry transcripts of his interviews. And me?"

A similar 'humm' was about to rise when the bus reached the stop where dragonflies flew down to rest. That was when the woman began running to catch the bus. The sight was indeed amusing. What a race! With a singular single jerk of the

2 the actress who usually plays the virtuous mother's role in Malayalam movies

3 a character artist who handles negative roles with ease, Lalitha was a member of the Kerala People's Arts Centre theatre academy

hand the *dupatta* sliding down the shoulder was put back in place, the folding umbrella was snapped close with a 'dup' sound and then she ran!

But he lost all interest and suddenly felt sleepy when he saw the woman running towards the bus he was traveling in. When a woman got into a bus, a clever sleep would overcome men traveling in seats reserved for women. He might be saved if he faked sleep. Or else, he would have to hang on to the bar till he reached Thrissur. What else could he do, but pretend sleep? But the woman didn't make him get up as Ajay feared. Instead, she came and sat in the vacant seat next to him without any hesitation. Suddenly his muscles contracted, not because he was shy of women. In fact, he had a superior kind of love for all women and possessed a smart heart that thumped while flirting with them. Still …

Ajay cocked his eyes and threw her a sideward glance. The sight was blurred as if he had opened his eyes under water. Suddenly he realized he didn't have to pretend to be asleep any longer. Also, he wasn't sure how long the woman would sit by his side. So, without wasting time he began to ogle her.

That afternoon he had preyed on his friend Sugunan for a few drinks. Ajay would become a different person at the window seat with some potent fluids within to flare up his imagination. He would usually become a magician who gave flight to the stars of his screenplays. But today, there was this woman beside him. Would she go away? He had heard that women didn't like the stench of liquor mixed up with sweat. And what if she got down four stops later at the Kottakkal bypass?

Soon Ajay opened his eyes and began surveying his fellow traveler. Good! A thoroughly sophisticated chic woman! Her skin was of golden hue. There wasn't an ounce of extra fat on the face or body.

That made him wonder what the celebrated movie director G.K. would have said about this woman. Of course, Ajay didn't know G.K. His friend Raghu who had just got a breather in movies, had talked about G.K.'s standard line on women who approached him for a role: "Good, good. Fine, there's no fat at all around the waist."

Ajay felt like laughing. The woman, however, unaware that the man next to her was a would-be director, began searching her handbag. She didn't realize that her dress had slid down revealing her shoulder bone and the strap of her inner garment. And that Ajay was feasting on that sight.

It was a beautiful round shoulder like the hump on a calf's back. Ajay couldn't take his eyes away from the smooth and fair skin of hers.

The woman didn't pay him any attention. She ignored him completely while taking out a lip balm and rubbing it on to her lips. Oh! What lovely lips! He wanted to see those ruby lips that were getting pampered. After closing the bag, she would deposit it in between them. Ajay knew it all so well.

That was the way women did things. When they had to sit next to strangers, the handbag would explain: 'Look we aren't related at all. We are complete strangers.'

"Where are you going?"

The woman didn't hear him and he was slightly embarrassed. She took out a wallet from the handbag, closed it and kept it on her lap. Ajay's handbag theory was proved wrong.

He peered at the currency note in her hand. If only he could make out the note's denomination, he would have known how long she would travel with him. But away from his sight she kept it folded in her palm.

She was leaning back in the seat, relaxed. Her posture was proud. Her profile was pretty. She had a restrained seriousness about her that gave hints of pedigree.

Her dress appeared different, turning dark blue towards the sides. That contrasted with her milky white complexion. She wore a gold chain of approximately 3 grams, and tiny ear studs.

The hair was tied up with a clip revealing a particularly beautiful neck – long and slender like that of foreigners without any scars or freckles.

However hard he tried he couldn't take his eyes off her. Like the innumerable crystals cracking up in saltpans, how many lines and squares and triangles on human skin!

Crystals cracking up in saltpans! Did he say that, Ajay wondered! What a distant simile of seashore! (He remembered

8

friend Sanal's criticism of his published short stories that they were full of rotten images of rural life. That was one reason he switched over to screenplays. Screenplays didn't need similes.)

He disentangled himself from the simile and looked again at his fellow traveler. She sat there folding the rupee in her hand once, and then again and then again. She looked like Indira Gandhi, absolutely unapproachable!

Fortunately, the bus took a sharp U-turn. She slid from her side of the seat and came and pressed onto him. Quite good a squeeze indeed!

'That's how it should be madam. It's God's will that we should share a bodily relation.' He told her inaudibly.

The bus was back on a straight path and the woman resumed her seat. Still he sat there repeating those lines to himself.

After a while the conductor came up to them. He stretched his hand towards the woman for money. She gave him the currency note in her hand muttering something. Despite straining to hear her words he couldn't make out her destination. Did the conductor hear her? The conductor took the note from her and looked at it once. Then he looked at the woman. He raised the note high for all to see it and asked: "Couldn't you have folded it once more, sister?"

Only then did the woman notice the sorry state of the currency note. It was folded like a beedi. She too laughed. Her smile bloomed gradually reminding Ajay of Preity Zinta, the Hindi actress with famous dimples. When she smiled, even the tip of her ears became red. Ajay felt like pinching her ears softly.

Don't pinch. He reminded himself. Anything could be termed an offense, even an affectionate pinch. A touch, for women, was a crime, and sometimes not touching too. Remember while traveling, sitting next to women or standing for that matter, a police station awaited you somewhere nearby.

After reading in the papers P.E.Usha's[4] harassment in a bus and its consequences, he got into a bus with trepidation. In fact when he said this to Sanal's wife, Meera, she had laughed out.

"Serves you right." Meera said breathlessly in between peals of laughter that rocked her whole body.

"Very good. Let all eve-teasers and roadside Romeos be taught a lesson."

Ajay Maneri got unreasonably angry. But he laughed and tried to look pleasant. The remnants of an unprofessed love for Meera still gleamed within.

"It's only our men who have this problem. There's no such harassment in other countries."

Winking at Sanal, Ajay provoked Meera: "Could it be that they lack libido there?"

---

4 PE Usha, an employee of the University of Kozhikode was sexually harassed in a local transport bus. The incident became a major controversy as it was followed by a vilification campaign by some pro-Left colleagues of the victim. Though Ms Usha was initially supported by women's organizations, ultimately her plight was no different from that of others who were ostracized for voicing their protest.

"Shut up." Meera got angry.

"Oh, as if you know all about the Whites! Do you know there is even a story about a White trying to touch a fellow woman traveler?" Sanal chipped in.

Ajay looked at Sanal with amusement and immediately he realized that it was a mistake. For Sanal's question came in thereafter: "Have you read it? It's called, I think, 'The adventure of a soldier." Before he could answer, came the refrain.

"Oh, it's in English. For the pre-degree exams didn't you answer the English paper in Malayalam!"

'And you were the one who evaluated my paper', Ajay wanted to reply but pretended as if he hadn't noticed Sanal's taunt.

"Who is the author?"

Sanal spelt out the name. He hadn't heard it before and couldn't make it out either.

Meera lowered her voice, and poking fun at her husband told Ajay: "Most probably there won't be any author by that name."

(Now, a short note from the author. This female character though pretty is utterly ignorant. There is a writer by that name: Italo Calvino. The name of the story is what Sanal said: *The Adventure of a Soldier*. It is a serious story about how Tomagra, a lonely and simple army man strives, desires and panics to touch a woman who sat next to him during his journey home on his first leave.)

On such occasions, Ajay used to feel that Meera had lost all her love for her husband and that she nurtured a secret love for him. And then, his love for her would soar as it usually did after a few drinks. Like two children sharing a secret, they began to laugh.

"What's it?"

Neither Meera nor Ajay answered Sanal's question. They stopped laughing. Suddenly Meera returned to the role of a housewife.

"Ajay, do you want some tea?"

Ajay replied without hiding his mounting love.

"Okay, then give me a cup of tea, dear. A cuppa that would sing your praises."

The fellow traveler's fall on to his shoulders interrupted his memories of love. He saw that she was asleep. That was a good sign. Now he could gawk at her with no qualms. When the bus fell into potholes, she deposited her body weight of 60-62 kg on him. For that very reason, Ajay didn't want to wake her up. Also, in those moments of physical contact he could get the faint fragrance of the perfume she had put on her inner garments: the scent of sweat and lavender. He pressed his nose to her shoulder and inhaled as much as he could. Sure, he was a bit coy of covertly enjoying the scent of the woman.

You might ask: Can't these guys, for heaven's sake, get married? My dear siblings, please try to understand one thing.

Should a man, who is unable to find his sustenance, get married and increase his own misery? Should he drag someone else into his misery? Tell me, please…

That greeting had come spontaneously. He congratulated himself for that wonderful piece of dialogue. What an apostrophe, sibling! If a popular actor repeated this some 10-20 times it could even become a Malayalam idiom.

Aha, what a sparkling gem of a piece of dialogue! He exclaimed and slapped the woman on the thigh. And then he realized the mistake and was horrified. No. She was still sleeping. That gave him some courage. For sheer fun, he left his palm to rest, as light as a feather, on her thighs. He waited. Nothing happened. Suddenly, he had a strange mysterious feeling that she was a lonely, helpless woman. Was she married? He searched for some signs like a *mangalsutra*, or *sindoor* on the forehead. He didn't find any. He sat watching her for sometime and then, he patted her thigh softly as if pressing on a loaf of bread. It felt like a bouncing rubber ball. Good. He was about to press her thigh once more. Then he had a doubt. Was she faking sleep? What if she was just waiting to see how far he would go and then create a scene, howling and hooting?

Ajay was scared and took his hand back. He stared at her again. But she didn't seem to be waking up. Or was she a flirt like Meera who enjoyed it all deep within, he wondered.

Meera was a great girl.

After their marriage, Sanal and Meera first visited Ajay when

13

his sister had just had her second baby. His siter's first born was bawling to seek attention, and the bride squatted on the floor with a toy car to entertain the child. He and Sanal were watching news on T.V. Then Ajay noticed that when Meera bent down, the rising mounds of her breasts were visible through her loose neckline. He could still remember the saffron-coloured *kameez,* its heart shaped neckline and the mesmerizing beauty of her yellow breasts, slightly pale, lacking suntan. The rounded curve and the largeness of the breasts swelling inside the clothes were enough to make even an impotent restless. He sat staring glued to her bosom. What would their tips be like? His X-Ray glare went far inside the neckline. When Meera raised her face once, she saw him ogling at her breasts. Suddenly she pulled her *dupatta* over her and grunted, 'Umm.' It was a scornful, "I see" meant to tell Ajay that she knew what he was up to.

Yet, it didn't seem like Meera had mentioned anything to her husband. They continued to invite Ajay to their place. And in the early days of their marriage, whenever he went there ostensibly to seek Sanal's help to stuff English words into his characters' mouths, all Ajay wanted was to see Meera. After a few drinks a visit to the Sanals would become an absolute necessity because it was then that his love for Meera would peak. She was the very embodiment of feminine charm. He hadn't seen another one like Meera.

But now one had to see to believe her plight. After nursing

her kids, her breasts hung loose inside her housecoat like two sagging bags of husk. The constant wiping of her dirty hands on the sides of the housecoat had turned the dress black.

Still, her face remained photogenic. With firm padded brassieres, a pair of navy blue jeans and striped T-shirt, she could still be transformed into the lead woman of TV soaps. The hit-maker of Malayalam TV, Shyam Sunder had actually worked out many such transformations.

Would the woman next to him be like Meera – playful, mischievous and forgiving of small indecencies? He wanted to make sure for himself. Ajay put his right hand into his trouser pocket as if to search for his wallet or spectacles and rubbed his elbow against the woman's breast. It was a difficult pose to retain for long; but he persevered. Feeling her with his elbow, he thought: This woman didn't seem to have had babies. Or, was it that she hadn't breast-fed them? Why was it so heavy? He knew well that this feat of his could earn him a slap on the face. So his first contact was very light, yet, he could feel the warmth and thrust of her left breast. The round and smooth female body hidden in clothing, he somehow felt was blending its breath and body warmth with his. He thought she was longing for a kiss. He sat looking at her resting body. She was leaning against him and he read into her body language the ecstasy of a woman enjoying a man's touch. That egged him on to more vulgarity. He removed his shoes and searched her feet. He wondered how her legs would be – the yellow thighs would have soft slanting golden hair like the veins on a leaf. A childhood fall could have left behind a greasy scar on her knee. It was a lecher's dream and he got a hard on at some critical juncture of his fantasy.

He couldn't make out what happened next. The woman woke up hissing like a snake. He was drenched in sweat as if he just had a heart attack.

He didn't know how to pretend like a man waking up from sleep. As if to find the man who troubled his fellow traveler he turned and looked back: An accusing, admonishing, warning look, meant to establish his innocence. Yet he couldn't face the woman. What if the glance she returned held bitterness, rebuke and contempt? Still, he managed to mutter, "What is it, what happened, sister?" She didn't say anything. His body was frozen. He felt thirsty like the one who had drunk an ocean. He couldn't sit there any longer. He got ready to get down seven or eight stops before his destination. When he got up, he felt wetness in his undergarment.

"Excuse me, sister, if you could please give me way, I could have got down."

The woman shifted her leg to a side, looked at him and smiled showing her dimples.

He couldn't believe himself as he stood waiting for the next bus. 'Was it really me, Ajay Maneri, who was so smutty to a woman? Was hers a knowing smile of someone who realized what I did to her?'

Suddenly he felt a genuine affection for that stranger. He asked her forgiveness on behalf of all the lewd men who at times lose themselves.

Could this have been the plight of the hero of the English story Sanal had told him?

However hard he tried he couldn't remember the name of the author. So he called him ... White, as in the outline stories with dots to be filled up which his mother made him write in his upper primary classes.

It was all right if Meera didn't want to read it. But he would ask Sanal to give him the book. Of course, it was difficult to understand an English story; still he should read it. At least he could find the similarities!

What Mother Ought to Know

Amma Ariyendathu

By Gracy

She blazed in the dark red sari. And while she stood wondering whether to plait her hair or tie it in a knot, the doorbell rang. Not able to decide, she left it open and answered the door. She laughed at her startled husband tottering backwards. There was fear in his eyes when he realized that the sharp edge of her laughter was boring open old wounds in his heart. In a feeble voice he reminded her, "You are going to mourn a death. It's your mother who is lying there dead."

She laughed out aloud. "What else should be celebrated but one's own mother's death?"

Like a soldier retreating from the front with wounds all over he walked towards the almirah. He chose a sari with printed yellow flowers and held it out to her. "I don't like the yellow colour at all," she spat out with contempt.

His visage grew miserable. She pulled out her bright red sari and hurled it on to the bed. She turned towards the mirror and stood staring at herself for a long while. Lost in some old memories she began to rub her face with trembling fingers. They crawled down her neck resting for a while on her small breasts. They stopped when they reached the underbelly. She then entwined her fingers, and tugging at them stretched her shoulders. She raised her face and yawned. He felt his wife more alien than ever before. He felt she would soon grow fangs and her tongue, dripping blood would jut out of her mouth.

But disproving his fear she took out a rose-coloured sari and wore it. She plaited her hair and casually put it forward. "I can't travel that far in a scooter. You better hire a taxi," she told him.

He stole a glance at his wife reclining on the back seat of the car. He couldn't understand how, suddenly, with the news of her mother's death the nervousness that had been stalking her these last three months slackened off. But then, did he know her at all? Why did this fair slender girl marry him of Stygian hue? Hadn't he been shocked at himself on the mirror? He was sure that she never loved him. She was always frigid in bed. He had tried in vain to rouse her with his hands and tongue.

His only comfort was the son she gave him. Every time his son, a medical student called up, he had wanted to ask whether a woman would lose herself at 41. But he regretted that there was never such camaraderie between him and the son. So he asked that question to himself, repeatedly. Earlier his fingers used to freeze when he touched her. But now a days he could hear something seething inside her. His hand stretched towards her to find out how it felt that moment.

Her eyes fluttered open to the touch. Her heart beat wildly in anticipation. She was impatient to see for herself and confirm mother's death. To mother, defiant and cheeky, death might have come dressed up as a magician. The permanent scorn that glossed mother's lips would have got evaporated at the touch of the magic wand.

Mother was proud of her genius that struck upon the simile of "two storks resting by the embankments of a paddy field" to describe her daughter's irregular incisors. She in turn was infuriated by mother's full round breasts that smiled condescendingly at the daughter's small bosom. Mother's black curls cascading down her back laughed out at her brownish hair of broom. The buttocks that spread their wings didn't even throw a glance at her backside. She had heard mother laughing under her breath about a black demon's proposal for the daughter. That very moment she decided, 'That demon will do for me!'

She got out of the car and went straight to the hall. Mother lay covered all over in her full stretch. She couldn't make out the changes that had come over mother the last five years. She sat beside the body and stared into its face. Mother had the face of someone who still hadn't got over the desire for life. The hue of cherry on her lips had faded out. She whispered keeping her face close to mother's ears, "At last you did lose your hold on everything, didn't you?"

She realized a ripple of laughter fleeting through the body. She trembled with rage. Grinding her teeth, she asked, "Can't you at least now put an end to all this?" Mother's eyes opened to draw a narrow line that let out an intense stare. Mother replied in a voice sharp as a needle, "No, I haven't decided to stop anything." She curled her lips, "Is it so? And just now you would turn into a handful of dust." Embers of laughter gleamed in mother's lips. "I'll be born again as your grandchild," mother said.

"All that should follow some frame of time and space. A spirit can't have its whims and fancies," she scoffed. Mother's face was contorted with determination. "Then you just wait and see. I will be born in your womb!" Suddenly she laughed out aloud in relief, "You old hag, this time you have been roundly beaten. I am past menopause already."

Then, all of a sudden, silence befell the murmuring at that house of mourning.

The Summons from God

Daivavili

By Sithara S

My parents' house had the scent of frankincense. There was a thick growth of dark green elephant ears, plantains and rubber saplings all around. Inside, my *ammachi* hurried about with some chore or the other. *Appachan* would either be out in the farm tending the plants or inside tallying the accounts of his grocery. Out in the stable, cows nodded their head to the smell of fried meat and dried fish from the kitchen. Upstairs, in my room in the afternoons, I lay asleep in the adolescent dreams of budding vines and blooming pomegranates – as in the Old Testament. Then, I was called Shirley.

I hadn't been there since I got converted. It was a year now. My husband Hari's mother was unlike *ammachi*. She didn't run around the house doing something, she didn't fry meat with coconut pieces, she didn't hum songs in the kitchen nor called out 'Shirley *mole*' in a musical tone. She called me Sita. In this last one year, she bought me many silk saris, *bindis* and small boxes to keep *sindoor*. She asked me to clean up the *pooja* room and light the lamp at dusk. She also taught me some prayers to be offered at that time.

Sometimes in the stillness of the *pooja* room, the lamp got blown off. The multi-coloured pictures of the deities, the camphor stand, the incense sticks and the matchboxes, all rocked in a silent dance. *Karthave,* Oh, my lord! I would let out a wail when the phlegm of fear clogged my heart.

After conversion, I thought of God with guilt. Yet, His thoughts made my mind cool and tender as if caressed by the gentle breeze from big trees. But then, the colourful faces in the pooja room would appear with all the intensity of the freshly revealed idol inside a sanctum sanctorum, plunging me into some mysterious gloom.

Sitting at The Soil Research Centre office canteen, over a cup of tea, I told all this to my colleague Mohammed. Our office was away from the city on the slope of a hill. Inside the huge boundary wall the long rows of lackluster buildings lay hidden among trees. A black, gleaming, tarred road trailed its way in the middle. Its black tributaries flowed in other directions. One such path led to this old canteen with tiled roof. Many of the employees, including Mohammed and me had our lunch and tea here. Each time we walked down this black path, sunlight stroked us wildly, sometimes wearily.

Mohammed tried to pacify me.

"You have been brought up in a certain set of beliefs. Now that they have changed, it is only natural that you have some problems."

He had told me something of this sort a year ago. That day, Hari was with us in this canteen. He was explaining that his mother would agree to our marriage only if I got converted. Or else the unmarried girls in his family would suffer, he said. The faith of our yet-to-be born children too hung in a balance.

I didn't protest. We were in love for five years. It felt so simple to me, like a funny game for the sake of others that would in no way harm my soul, heart or life.

Sipping a mouthful of hot tea, I coughed with force. It was some days since I began coughing. Even as a kid I had asthma. Skeins of sputum blocked my windpipe emptying the air out of my chest. All through the night I would cough thirsting for some oxygen. *Ammachi* would get up from her sleep to make me black coffee with pepper, dried ginger and small onions. Then *appachan* and *ammachi* would take me to the prayer room. I used to whimper the prayers of faith heeling along with them. After sometime, the kind eyes of Jesus would extend like a tube and suck out all the sputum from my chest.

After our marriage Hari took me to several doctors. But none of them had those eyes filled with kindness. At night I lay breathless beside a sleeping Hari. The prayers for the ill choked in my throat like the oxygen that dodged me.

"Shirley ... Sita, are you all right?" Mohammed asked. He looked sorry for calling me Shirley. He was wondering whether he had offended me. I had seen this worry in many of my friends' faces. But even after a year, I wasn't fully aware that I was now Sita. I startled still when I heard someone call me Sita. My mind then, scared of the loss, chanted Shirley ... Shirley.

I coughed again. Traces of *sindoor* fell on my hand. Hari's mother never let me step out without *sindoor* on my forehead. Even if I were home and had forgotten to put it on, a stern reprimand filled her eyes. Once she turned emotional, explaining that the blood-coloured sindoor was the symbol of strength and prosperity and that a Hindu woman ought to be proud sporting it. That reminded me of a woman who as a penalty for her wanton ways was forced to walk the streets with a scarlet letter on her forehead. Still I had to bear this burden on my head.

Our tea was over for some time now. "Let's take a walk instead of going back to the office now," Mohammed said. We took the wicket gate by the side of the canteen and walked slowly towards the hilltop in the soft sun.

The trees all round stood still. There were tufts of green grass along the path. On the sides, beyond the hedges we saw tiled chimneys rising from the houses.

At the hilltop we sat under a big tree. The climb had worsened my cough, leaving me breathlessness. The power of the phlegm that cloaked my chest like fungus shook my body violently. I became aware of a frightening vacuum filling the airless tubes and chambers of my throat and chest. My eyes overflowed. I muttered with closed eyes and a fluttering throat:

There's no misery in this path where Jesus reigns ...

You will find no injustice in His trail ...

Watch over me, giving me strength, oh! Jesus ...

It was sunset. *Appachan* had returned from the grocery shop. "Shirley *mole*, get up, its time for prayer." *Ammachi* was calling out. They knelt down in their small chapel before lit candles. Lizy *chechi* who had joined the convent and become a nun had also come. Lizy *chechi* led the prayer in a voice that could melt even the stonehearted. *Ammachi* and *appachan* were repeating after her in soft and harsh voices. The scent of frankincense filled the room. The candle flames were reflected on the picture of Jesus that hung before them. On His smiling face was the graceful tranquil glow of love.

When I opened my eyes, I saw Mohammed's face filled with compassion. "Don't worry, Sita", he said in a soft voice. "No, not Sita, Shirley." I smiled at him. His hands slipped into mine. His lips touched lightly on the hollow of my gasping throat. His eyes closed coupling with my dried out eyes. His meandering tongue erased the *bindi* from my throbbing forehead. The red powder at the parting of my hair was on his lips. He moved my gold chain and the *mangalsutra* to one side and gently caressed my chest inflamed with the innumerable strands of sputum. I lay exhausted in his arms waiting for the breath of life.

All around us were the huge trees touching the skies, nurtured by the magic of earth. Trees that broke into buds at a touch of dampness, whose leaves gleamed like metal tablets and branches murmuring something. Suddenly they blew a breeze. Fresh, green oxygen, cool and pristine, like the stream that flowed down from the mountain crest; I saw it drifting like tiny pieces of glass. Hungrily, I drew it in and its touch melted the warm clots of phlegm away. My heart leapt up with verve and the nostrils throbbed in a pleasurable numbness. My body turned into a pulsating dance hall.

After a while when we walked down the hill I told Mohammed that he should speak to the office superintendent and get me a week's leave. I wanted to go home with Hari. Then I took his mobile phone and called up Hari at home. I told him that I was going to reconvert to become Shirley again, and that he should come with me to visit my parents the next day. I switched off the phone without waiting for his reply.

When we went down the narrow path along the hill slope, Mohammed stopped to show me something. Beyond the bushes was a crater that looked as if the earth had split into two. It must have happened in some landslide. Holding tightly on Mohammed's hand I peered into it. A narrow tunnel to earth's womb! My heart turned bitter with certain ancient memories. I coughed up the remaining clot of phlegm from my chest and spewed it into that slit.

The Perfect Wife

*Ellam Thikanja Bharya**

By K. Saraswathi Amma

Divakaran Nair had started his hunt for a wife when he was 20. He had certain set ideas of how his future wife should be. She should be 14 years old, should have a golden complexion, long wavy curls which fell down to her knees and eyes that remained glued to the ground. However, she should have a face that could attract anyone who happened to look at her. She shouldn't be more than five feet tall and should have a lovely body. He never thought that an illiterate woman could not be good wife material. In fact, how gratifying would it be to a husband to pour out his knowledge and refinement to an ignorant little girl in his free time!

Divakaran Nair's outlooks didn't change even when he turned from a handsome youth to a middle-aged man with patches of grey hair. A maiden past her 15th year was an old hag in his eyes; if a woman didn't have a complexion to match the gold she wore, he thought of her as jet black. He believed that any girl who had studied till fourth form was of dubious character.

While in college, Divakaran Nair used to wonder about his friends who were busy seeking love. Divakaran Nair had only disdain for the girls in his college. He considered them not less that prostitutes. What prompted them to roam around all over the place without the cover of a male body? Didn't the beauty and allure of womanhood lie in not being revealed?

One day Divakaran Nair's bicycle hit an Intermediate student. His cycle toppled down along with her. He told the girl who had sat up and was trying to lift up her heavy body from the ground.

"My dear sister, you shouldn't have done this in the middle of the road in broad daylight. I would have come to your house if you had told me earlier. I have that much chivalry in me."

"Oh, so your sisters are of those kind?" she retorted. As she picked up her books and walked away, he said to himself.

"She too is a woman? How could she look into a man's face and say this? Shameless eunuch."

It was around this time that his friend Ramakkuruppu decided to get married. Divakaran Nair tried his best to dissuade his friend when he came to know that the bride was doing a course in lab technology. "What would your marriage be worth if your wife is not like Sitadevi and Sheelavathi who considered their husbands God? Do you think your wife will swear by whatever you say? She will quote 300 examples from America, Europe and even Russia to prove you wrong. How will you bear it? Moreover, in her eyes even for a second you wouldn't be transformed into a magician who could create for her a sweet miraculous world. Instead, what blissful joy you would feel when a little girl blessed with ignorance stands before you helpless as if she has lost her consciousness with your first touch! God! You are losing out on that ecstasy. What charm will you find in a woman who has mingled with other men, who doesn't have any shame to stand before your friends? That marriage will make you an ascetic. So ..."

When Divakaran Nair's lecture reached this point Ramakkuruppu took out the invitation cards from the drawer of his table and began to write addresses on them.

Even the attendants of the lodge they stayed in went for the wedding, but Divakaran Nair refused to go. That unusually silent night brought crystal clear images of his dream bride. Every morning he used to make coffee for himself, leave it at the bedside stool and curl up in the bed again. He got up after a while to have the coffee, so that he would get the feel of bed-coffee in its real term. Marriage would put an end to this humiliating practice. After an amorous night when he would wake up in the morning hearing the jingle of bangles, he would see a shyly smiling enchanting face. Sitting on the bed that still retained her body's warmth, he would take the cup of coffee from her lotus-like hands and slowly sip it as if tasting divine nectar.

He never thought that the woman in his dreams was unattainable. Many nights, when his friends wandered around searching for pleasure, he would lie in his bed imagining his married life. Unlike other men, he treasured his virginity to gift it to his 14-year-old perfect wife. Each night he would fall asleep thinking of how he would brush back the dark curls from her forehead, her head bent with shyness and he gazing into that beautiful face.

He was also interested in all the material things that a woman desired. Whenever he saw new ornaments Divakaran Nair would copy that design and the jeweler's address in his diary. When he happened to see fashionable new sari blouses he would decide which design to select for his wife.

Divakaran Nair had indeed found a perfect girl in his early days of wife-hunting. He had gone home for Christmas vacation and was dumbfounded when he saw Kalyanikutty at the gate of Malayalam Middle School. He was determined to marry her though he came to know that her father was a lower grade government employee and that she was the eldest of his many children. But what more did a woman need other than the riches of beauty and the ornament of coyness?

The day he went to see Kalyanikutty at her home, he was received like a king. Her father escorted her to the front room while her mother sat in the kitchen promising the most tantalizing offerings to all the gods. It was for the first time that Kalyanikuyy's body was being exhibited as a commodity to be desired and chosen. More than being bashful, she was curious. So she raised her face and looked at Divakaran Nair while placing the plate of snacks before him. It was a major blow to Divakaran Nair who had been gazing at her elated. What pleasure could he expect from being the husband of a girl who didn't mind looking at a stranger's face in her 14th year? Divakaran Nair didn't even touch the snacks Kalyanikutty brought for him.

Still, he couldn't help heaving a deep sigh when he heard two months later that she had been married off to a lame munsif court clerk. That was not because he regretted not marrying Kalyanikutty, but because he was reminded of her audacity that made her look straight on his face.

Divakaran Nair didn't notice the years passing by, making 14 year olds 18, 20 and 28 year olds. When he looked into the mirror he used to feel proud of his handsome looks. But now, he began to feel troubled. Earlier he used to take not more than half an hour to comb his hair. Now even one hour was not enough to pluck out the grey hairs. Somebody told him that it was because of his failing health that his legs ached when he cycled for a while. Theses days he wasn't very keen to make coffee in the mornings either, still he couldn't stop that habit. "For how long will this go on?" His body beginning to lose its youth would ask his heart at times. But his still youthful and continued to lure him with the image of a beautiful face.

Then one day, he got a letter from Pankajakshiamma. Divakaran Nair felt relieved reading the letter.

'*Chetta*, you should come here immediately. I have selected a girl for you. Her name is Kamala. You just have to come here, meet her parents and take her with you.'

If Pankajakshi felt so, Kamala should be a perfect girl, he decided.

As he sat looking at the beautiful handwriting he felt gratitude and sympathy for the writer of that letter who clearly sounded anxious for his well-being.

Pankajaksiamma was his father's niece. Though she was not pretty, her proposal too had come for Divakaran Nair as she was his *murappennu*[1].

"I do like Panku, poor soul. But liking somebody and marrying her are two different things. How could anyone look lovingly at a dark ghoul like her and consider her his wife?"

Pankajakshiamma too came to know about his comment. But she was well aware of her ugly looks and so didn't nurse any ill feelings against Divakaran Nair for his logical sarcasm. Their friendship continued unabated. Pankajakshi did her matriculation and became the wife of an Ayurveda *vaidya* and soon became a widow. She got a job in a nearby school for the sake of her children. Often, Divakaran Nair helped her financially though it meant cutting into the savings he had kept aside for his future.

---

1 uncle's (mother's brother) daughter whom the Malayalee Hindu is entitled to marry.

He never expected any returns. Still, only Pankajakshiamma could search out the thing he aspired to possess, wasting a good 15 years of his life. Of course, he had never lost hope even once.

The moment he saw Kamala he felt that his life had been fulfilled. The bride of his dreams was standing before him just as he had imagined her to be. He wanted to enfold that slender body in his arms and whisk her away that very moment. When she disappeared inside the house he forgot all about the coffee she had brought and sat there lost in dreams, his hand to his chin.

Her father mistook that blissful reverie for disappointment. He tried to guess the reason behind it and consoled him.

"Don't consider her thin figure. Of all our children, she alone has completely taken after her mother. Do you know what her mother looked like when I married her? She was as thin as a palm leaf. She had the same complexion and built as this girl. People who had seen her then won't recognize her now. She has put on so much weight. Once she sits on the floor she has to support herself on both her hands to get up. And her complexion? Now she is the colour of lemon. Good ripe lemon. So, please don't be disheartened by how Kamala looks now. If she has enough to eat, she will get fat within two days." He laughed out aloud. "It would be better if you get a new wider door for your house."

He expected his wife's appreciation for his eloquence and peered into the house. Divakaran Nair didn't hear anything of his terrible concept of beauty, as he was busy making plans for the honeymoon.

When the daughter went inside the house, the mother walked to the front room to see the candidate. She hid behind the door and peeped out holding her youngest baby at her breast to feed him. The moment she saw Divakaran Nair, she recognized the man who had for the first time roused in her virgin heart hopes of a married life. She had become quite loud-mouthed over the years.

"*Ayyayyo*! Is this the man? Wonderful! Are you still going around houses searching for a bride and drinking coffee? See, I have become the mother of eight children. And have turned into an old woman."

Divakaran Nair got to his feet in a panic and looked at the snow mountain standing before him. She looked at her confused husband and continued:

"We don't need this alliance even if he promises to shower us with gold. Chi! It's so shameful. The same man who had come with a proposal for the mother has now come seeking the daughter's hand! Would anyone give him a girl? If Pankajakshiamma had told me that his pastime is going around gaping at girls, I wouldn't have agreed to this humiliating affair. What a waste when there's not enough to spend on sugar and coffee! Anyway, now that it's all over, you just get off from here. The children will have the coffee.

Divakaran Nair walked away with a bent head. He was not sure what caused him more pain – Kalyanikuttyamma's harsh words or the changes that had come over her beautiful body.

That day, his sleeping desires pivoted on an ideal wife were kindled beyond control. The mind could be assuaged with the diversion of dreams, but what about the body?

The next morning he took the cup of coffee from Pankajakshiamma's rough hands with a new resolution. He could hear her children playing outside. Divakaran Nair discovered that the dark fat body of that teacher fulfilled all his concepts of a perfect wife though he had nothing new to teach her.

---

* The copyright of the Malayalam story rests with DC books, Kottayam

Smell of a Bird

Pakshiyude Manam

By Madhavikutty

A week after reaching Calcutta, she saw the advertisement in a newspaper. 'Wanted: a good-looking, efficient young woman to be in charge of our wholesale department. She should have an understanding of colours and new designs. Contact our office with a hand-written application.'

The office was in a crowded street. It was 11 when she reached the office building. She wore a pale yellow sari and carried a white handbag. It was a huge building with seven floors, over 200 rooms and many verandahs. There were four lifts with a massive crowd in front of each one. There were portly traders, and office-goers holding leather bags. She couldn't spot another woman anywhere there. Then she began losing her confidence. She shouldn't have come here against her husband's words. She asked an office boy who stood next to her:

"Where is the textile company's office?"

"I think it's in the first floor." He said. She felt all eyes on her. She shouldn't have come. Why did she come at all into the midst of these sweating men? Even if the company gives her a thousand rupees she wouldn't be able to come here daily ... But, she couldn't give up that easily.

Her turn came. She got into the lift and stood cringing in a corner trying not to touch others.

She got down at the first floor and looked around. There were doors to each room along a corridor that stretched on all four directions. Each door had a name board outside such as 'Export and Import' and 'Wine sellers'. She passed many rooms and their name boards, but still couldn't find the one she was searching for. Her palms started sweating. Suddenly a man came out of a room and she asked him:

"Where is the textile company's office?"

The man with his narrow red eyes scanned her from head to toe.

"I don't know. But if you come with me I will ask the office boy and let you know."

He was a short, middle-aged man. There was dirt under his fingernails. May be that put her off, she didn't feel like going with him. She said:

"Thanks, I'll find it myself."

She walked fast and turning a corner reached another corridor. There too she saw large shut doors. A board hung there, which read 'Dying'. She laughed at the way it was spelt out. Do people die here or are clothes dyed? Anyway, she decided to check out the office and pushed the door open. Inside, she saw a big empty hall. There were 2-3 chairs and a glass-topped table. That was all. There was no one there. She asked aloud:

"Anybody there?"

A curtain on a door that opened to a room inside, stirred a bit. She mustered courage and went and sat in the chair in the middle of the room. She couldn't take another step without resting for a while. A ceiling fan went on above her head. What sort of an office was this? She wondered. Where had everyone gone keeping the doors open and the ceiling fan on?

Since they were dyers, they would know where she should go. She took out a little mirror from her handbag and touched up her face. Should she demand Rs 800? They would think it lucky to have an employee like her. She was a learned woman, had a good social standing and having traveled abroad even knew the world.

She woke up to the sound of a bottle being uncorked. What a fool was she! She had dozed off in this strange place! She rubbed her eyes and looked around.

A young man sat opposite her pouring soda into his whisky. He wore a butter-coloured terylene bush shirt. There was a healthy growth of body hair on his hand from his finger upwards. Looking at those powerful fingers she suddenly panicked. Why did she come to this Satan's abode?

He raised his head and looked at her. His face was long like that of a horse. He asked: "Did you sleep well?"

Then without waiting for her reply he raised his glass and gulped down the liquid.

"Are you thirsty?"

She shook her head.

"Do you know where the textile company is? I thought you would know. You people dye clothes, don't you?" She smiled courteously. He didn't smile. He poured whisky into the glass again, and mixed soda. It was as if they had all the time in the world to talk.

"Don't you know?" She was getting impatient now. She felt like getting out of that place somehow and going back home.

Suddenly he laughed out. His lips were very narrow. It made his laugh grotesque.

"What's the hurry? Its only 11.45."

She walked towards the door.

"I thought you would know." She said. "I thought you were associated with the textile trade."

"What association? We do not dye clothes. Didn't you read the board outside, Dying?"

"That means ...?"

"Yes, it means what it says. Haven't you heard of dying? We facilitate good peaceful death."

He winked leaning back on the chair, and looked at her laughing. Suddenly she felt his pale laugh spreading into her eyes. She felt weak in her knees.

She ran towards the door. But her sweating hands couldn't open it. Tears welled up in her eyes.

"Please open the door." She said. "I have to reach home. My children must be waiting for me." She thought hearing her he would forego his malicious designs and would help her.

"Please open the door." She pleaded. He took a swig of the drink once and then again. And laughed out repeatedly looking at her.

She started knocking on the door. "Are you trapping me in here?" She asked loudly. "What wrong did I do to you?"

Her sobs subsided after a while. Exhausted, she fell on the floor next to the door.

He kept on saying something in a soft voice without even a trace of harshness. Some of his words fell into her ears.

"Long ago during the winter, a bird got trapped in my bed room. It was brown in colour, with a tinge of yellow — exactly the colour of your sari. It tried to knock at the glass windows. It tried its best to break open the window fluttering its wings. But what happened, then? It fell down tired. I crushed it under my boots."

After a pause of a few moments he asked again:

"Do you know what the smell of death is like?"

She looked up at him. She wanted to tell him something, but her words got trapped in her mouth. Who would know the scent of death or rather the different scents of death better than her? It had the smell of rotting wounds, the sweet smell of orchards, smell of incense sticks ...

In a small dark room, lying on the bed spread on the bare floor her mother used to tell her in a voice devoid of all dignity.

"I am sick, dear ... there is no pain. But, I am not well ..."

Fat white worms writhed in the wounds of her mother's leg. Still she said: "I don't feel any pain ..."

Then it was her father's turn. When her diabetic father fainted suddenly she felt a breeze waft in from the orchard. Sweet was the smell that spread inside the room, but that too was death ...

She wanted to tell him all this. But her tongue had lost its power.

The young man sitting in the middle of the room went on saying:

"You don't know, do you? I'll tell you. Death has the smell of a bird's feathers. You will discover it very soon. Do you want to find it straight away? What is your favourite hour of the day? Is it the time when the earth lay shamelessly naked while the sun looked on right from the top? Or is it the dusk? What sort of a woman are you? Courageous or cowardly?"

He stood up and walked up to her. He was very tall. She said:

"Let me go. I never intended to come to this place."

"No, you're lying. How many times you had decided to come here! How many times have you wished for a happy ending! Aren't you like a river that yearns to plunge indolently and get assimilated into the ocean that lies sighing deeply, full of soft waves? Tell me. Darling, don't you want to feel that final caress?"

"Who are you?" She sat up. She felt an eerie attraction in his fingers.

"You haven't seen me?"

"No."

"I have come to you many times. Once when you were just eleven. You were in bed, sick with jaundice; you couldn't even raise your head from the bed. When your mother opened the windows, you said: 'Mother, I see yellow flowers. Yellow oleanders. It is yellow flowers everywhere ...' Remember?"

She nodded her head.

"I was amid those yellow flowers that only you could see. I was waiting to hold your hands and take you where you wanted to go ... But, you didn't come that day. You weren't aware of my love. You didn't know that I was yours and everyone else's guide."

"Love! Is this love?" She asked.

"Yes, only I can reveal love in all its perfection. You will offer me everything one by one ... Your rosy lips, your eyes of a doe, your beautiful body...even each of your body hair ... Everything will cease to be yours. In return for this sacrifice, I will give you freedom. You will become nothing, but everything. You will be there in the surging sea waves, you will stir in the old trees growing fresh buds in the rains, your wail will rise along with the sobs of the seeds that lie in labour in earth's womb. You will become the wind, the rain drops, the tiny grains of sand ... you will become the beauty of this world ..."

She stood up. She felt that she had gotten over her fatigue finally. With a new found courage she said: "All this must be true. But you have rounded up the wrong person. I am only 27. I am married. I have kids. My time hasn't come yet. I came here looking for a job. Now it must be 12.30. Let me go back home."

He didn't say anything. He allowed her to open the door and go out. She walked around looking for a lift. She felt that her footsteps were resounding loudly all around.

When she reached the lift, she stopped. There was no operator in the lift. Still, she got into it, and shut the door. She pressed the switch. It rose up suddenly with the initial hum of a collapse. She felt she was in the skies and she could hear the thunder. That was when she saw the board hanging inside the lift: "Danger. Lift on repair."

Then, darkness spread – a resonating, roaring darkness. She never had to get out of it again.

Madness

Bharanthu

By B M Suhra

The alarm clock as usual woke her up early in the morning. She didn't feel like getting up. It hurt as if slashed with a blade all over. She felt the weight of a huge rock in her head. It had been some days since she began feeling unwell. Yet, when the alarm went off, she always dragged herself out of the bed. But today somehow, she just couldn't leave her bed. What would happen if she didn't? Would the earth stop moving in its orbit? She curled up, pulling the blanket over her.

Her husband was startled at the non-stop ringing of the alarm. He woke up, turned off the alarm and shook her shoulders trying to wake her up.

"Get up. The alarm had gone off long ago!

"You get up."

She turned her back to him.

The husband got up and put on the light. He pulled her blanket away.

"Get up and make some tea."

"I told you I won't."

He was taken aback at her belligerence.

His voice turned harsh.

"I asked you to get up and make tea."

"And didn't you hear me saying no? Stop getting on to my nerves and go make it yourself."

She shouted at her husband who stood flummoxed looking at her.

"Didn't you hear me? Go to the kitchen."

Not able to confront her glare he walked to the kitchen. She guffawed in pure joy.

Why didn't she do this even once in the last 15 years? She pulled the blanket over and went back to sleep. In her dreams she saw a colorful world. One had to be really lucky to lie idle like this in a cold morning.

"Tea?"

"Keep it there."

She ordered, half asleep.

Her husband kept the cup of tea on the side-table and left in a huff. She slowly stepped into the bathroom, brushed her teeth, washed her face and had tea at leisure. She had never got time to enjoy her morning tea. The tea was not bad. Was it a bit too sweet?

Then it was okay. She had almost forgotten the days

when she had her morning cuppa in bed. When she was in college her mother used to wake her up with a cup of piping hot tea.

She felt rejuvenated with the tea and walked up to the verandah. Her husband sat there sour-faced, reading the newspaper. She turned red seeing him.

"Well, are you still sitting here reading the newspaper? Haven't you been to the kitchen yet? Don't you know that the school bus comes at 8 o'clock?"

He stared at her. She didn't budge. She snatched the paper away and said:

"There is *puttu* flour in the cup board and some bananas. You fry a few papads."

"I don't know how to make *puttu*."

"What about omelet then?"

"Um."

"Fine. Bread and omelet will do for today. But from tomorrow, try and learn to make something better."

He stood dazed.

"Don't stand here with a blank face. Go fast and buy a loaf of bread. Buy some plantains too. You can steam them."

She laughed out aloud when he went in silently to put on his shirt. Walking out with a bag to the shop, he looked back at her in suspicion several times. When he returned, she was in the armchair reading the newspaper.

After she was through with the newspaper she felt like taking a bath.

The morning shower always made her feel fresh. While in college, she began her studies after an early morning bath. Now after all her morning chores it would be mid-noon when she found time to bathe. The water in the overhead tank would be boiling under the scorching sun and after the bath she felt more exhausted.

She hummed a tune and walked in to see her husband sitting by the telephone and leafing through the directory. It's quite a task to search a number in it.

"Haven't you been to the kitchen yet? Did you give the children tea? Keep your phone calls for the evening or you would be late for office. I am going to have a bath."

She pushed and shoved her husband who stood rooted to the kitchen. She felt like sitting on the chair from where she dragged him away and make a call to someone. But who to call? She didn't have any friends in this city. Her mother, these days was hard of hearing. She went to the bathroom and switched the geyser on. She rubbed her husband's herbal oil all over her body. She massaged her scalp with another oil preparation. While the water was getting hot she worked out a bit. Then she poured cold water over her head till she felt refreshed.

She washed her body with warm water and scrubbed off the oil. After the bath she pampered her body with talcum powder, changed into a well-ironed sari and blouse and combed her hair. She saw a different person in the mirror. She put kohl in her eyes and a bindi on her forehead and enjoyed herself once again in the mirror. Not bad. Not bad at all! She didn't look her 35 years. As she stood there she felt like singing. She used to sing well in college. Even now her voice was good. Humming a love song she reached the door. But someone had locked it from outside. Who? Why did he lock her up in the room?

She listened to what was going on outside with her ear on the door. He was talking on the phone.

"Hello, Murthy, it's me, Raghavan. Please come here fast. I don't know what has happened, my wife is not well since morning. It's rather strange, she has become a bit violent. She had never uttered a word against me in 15 years. But this morning she became a completely changed person. She behaves as if she is settling scores with me. I am really scared. I think we will have to take her away forcibly. Send an ambulance. Get someone to assist you. I might have to admit her in the hospital. Come fast ... I am very scared. No, I have locked the room. Don't worry. Just come fast."

She couldn't hear anything more. She hit her head on the door and screamed.

"Open the door. I am okay ... Open the door ... I am all right. I did it for fun ... Please open the door. I have to get to the kitchen. Open the door ... Please!"

Maanikkan

By Lalithambika Antharjanam

Their joy knew no bounds. After months of pleading and urging, the two kids of that shack had just got a calf to keep. Azhakan, the boy ran up to give it a big hug.

"What a lovely calf, its mine ..."

"Aiyya! No way, Appan has already asked me to fetch grass for it." Neeli, established her right. Azhakan would not give up. "Why do you need a he-calf? After all, I have to plough the field with it when it grows up into a bull. Buffaloes and bulls are not meant for girls. You can keep your hens and ducks."

"Big deal ..." Neeli sulked. "I don't want your bull and plough. You better take care of it yourself, if you have to plough the field with it."

Their father, Karumban who was listening to their argument intervened at that moment:

"Stop it kids. Neeli, you fetch it some water to drink. You get some grass for it, Azhakan"

The quarrel ended there. In the evening the kids built a small shelter for the calf. It was not a stable, nor a shed. Right at the back of their hut, a little mansion made of grass and cane. At one side were the manger and the small stump; the ground was leveled and smoothened with a knife. It was neater and tidier than their own little shack. Azhakan laid a bed of hay, Neeli came with a tub of water for it. Their guest getting weary of this indulgence blinked its eyes and chewed the cud.

In these one and a half years of its life, this was the only time it ate its fill. It was born in the master's *pucca* cattle shed made of bricks. The strength of the mother cow's milk showed on the master's children. Vellamma cow gave five litres of milk every day. Yet, her son grew thinner by the day. And when the calf was all skin and bones and almost dead, the compassionate master remembered Karumban's request.

"If you could give me a calf to look after ... My children were very keen ..."

The request was granted. Karumban was a loyal servant. His ancestors had served the house for four generations. But none had ever got a favour of this sort granted by the master. Karumban was beside himself with joy. He carried that calf all the way home. Even if it could have walked, he would not have put it down.

Karumban, the doting father, was delighted. His children's dreams have come true.

That night Azhakan and Neeli quarreled again – about a name

for their calf. It should be the loveliest of all names they knew.

"What is Chothi's calf called? Yes, Maniyan. We will also call ours, Maniyan," Neeli said.

"Stupid, isn't that a buffalo?" Azhakan was angry again. "This is a bull, with even a white mark on its forehead." For him a bull was much superior to a buffalo. Though it was just a matter of names, it was highly inappropriate to give them a similar treatment.

"What about the master's big bull that pulls a cart? That white one ... what is its name?"

Azhakan thought for a while and said: "Oh, I got it ... Maanikkan – Maanikkan! That would do for our calf too ..."

Karumban who was half asleep was woken up by the kids' fuss. "What are you now fighting for? Maanikkan or Maniyan, decide fast and go off to sleep."

The calf was baptized that auspicious hour – Maanikkan! Neeli's grass and water and Azhakan's nurture helped Maanikkan grow up. What a tame calf it was! The kids would touch and hug it, they would adorn its small horns with tender palm leaf, put a garland of *kunnikuru* around its thickening chin and if a little dung somewhere soiled its glimmering torso, they washed it off that very moment.

During the next harvest season, with the money they saved up gathering and selling loose paddy, the kids bought Maanikkan a small bronze bell. They had seen such a bell on the master's Maanikkan. The day they put the bell around its neck, they led Maanikkan into the neighbourhood. Let them turn green! Nowhere far and wide were such a bronze bell and such a gorgeous calf.

One, two, three – years passed by. Maanikkan grew up. Now he was fit to plough the field. Azhakan became a farmer. On the day of *Vishu*, for the first time, Azhakan led Maanikkan to the field with a lighted lamp and a *nirapara*. Karumban watched on with joy. His son and the calf they brought up had come of age. Both were smart and sturdy. What more to achieve!

To begin with Maanikkan did not know how to pull the plough. It would run wild or stand and hesitate. But the moment Azhakan's stick rose in the air, Maanikkan would move on like a scared child, head bent and tail wagging. Only once was the stick brought down. But the very memory of that led the dignified Maanikkan the right way.

Azhakan wouldn't have a drop of water before feeding Maanikkan. He would look on lovingly, as the bull after filling its stomach, chewed the cud in the shade of trees. His glance, bright and happy surpassed that of the groom who gazed at his newly wed wife. His Maanikkan, his companion, his friend, his life …

"I could get my fill just watching Maanikkan." He used to tell Neeli. That was true. Anyone who saw Maanikkan would feel delighted.

The colour was a light brown with a tinge of red. It had

well spread out horns and a sturdy, fleshy body – a perfect handsome bull. Some said the length of its tail meant an unruly temperament. Between the forelegs was a big white mark that spread up to its neck. This only added to its beauty. Its gait was a head-turner. Stamping the hoofs, swaying all over – there was not a piece of cattle like Maanikkan in the whole village, and a farmhand like Azhakan. And the rest of the village envied the master, for his produce was increasing day by day.

Maanikkan was smart but mischievous. It would poke every other piece of cattle in the field with its horns. None had its strength. But for Maniyan, Chothi's buffalo, no one would even go near it. And the Maanikkan – Maniyan pair bagged all the prizes at farm contests. But only Azhakan was fortunate to receive those prizes. Once Maanikkan was in the field with the yoke and the nose string, it would bellow and sway its big horns at all other farmhands who approached it. Other workers could not stand it, Chothi in particular. 'Was not this act specially tutored by Azhakan?' Chothi would think. Azhakan and Chothi were of the same age, they grew up together, were the same master's slaves. His own buffalo and Azhakan's bull formed one pair. Did not half the pride go to him, and also the master's good will that went with it?

Maanikkan's fame spread far and wide. Traders stepped in with their quotes – fifty, sixty, hundred, two hundred. Azhakan was shocked. It was then that he realized that Maanikkan was a piece of cattle, a thing that had to change many hands. After all, it belonged to someone else.

But ... Why should he bother at all? If this bull was sold another would be bought and tilling would go on. He would be the one to use that bull too. Then, what was so special about Maanikkan? Bulls were just animals that were to be used to plough the land. They were not pets. They were commodities to be sold and bought for the profit they would bring in. Azhakan knew all this. Still his heart throbbed for Maanikkan.

Some cruel farmer or hauler would buy Maanikkan and overwork it. Maanikkan was not used to hard labour. On its own Maanikkan did four bulls' work. But who cared for that? Azhakan knew how cruel the workers were, how they treated their ever-sorrowful companions.

After a good day's work what Maanikkan wanted was some rest. Azhakan had seen cattle with long deep wounds on both sides of their torsos. Once when Enathi's ox faltered in the field the farm labourers rubbed chilly powder into its eyes. He had seen things like stuffing a lit match into the nostrils of a bull, bending and breaking the tail and worse. If someone did like this to Maanikkan ... *Ayyo*! The very thought broke Azhakan's heart. He would pray out aloud unaware of where and with whom he was:

"*Karimala Chathave*[1]! I would make an offering of crackers if no one comes with a suitable price for Maanikkan."

It seemed like Azhakan's trick of bribing the Sastha worked,

---

1 a tribal God

70

the master demanded a huge price for Maanikkan. No one would pay the price of an elephant for a bull, however great it be. Thus, the fear of parting faded away.

The maiden harvest was over. It was sowing time and the whole village came alive. The big day of sowing arrived. There were lots of people to watch the now-famous Maanikkan run the race. Only Azhakan could handle the plough matching its swiftness. But when it was time to take Maanikkan out, Chothi had a wish:

"Friend, it's you who hold the plough always. Today let me do it. Let me hold the plough for Maanikkan."

Azhakan complied. It was a valid request. He set Maanikkan on the field along with its pair, patted it encouragingly and drew back. Chothi took over the plough. A smile of gratitude filled his face.

Maanikkan pounced forward tinkling the bell. Farmers who were watching on the banks hollered with excitement. What a roar it made ... Like rushing waves, Maanikkan ran fast splashing muddy water all around. Chothi's delight knew no bounds. He ran after them swirling his rod.

He shouted the primitive shriek of a worker's thrill and in this excitement he unknowingly lowered the rod in his hand. It was a common thing – the bull must be walking on but still villagers could not help hitting it. Chothi was no different. But Maanikkan was a different bull. It was not used to ill treatment. Agitated by the unexpected lash, the bull turned around. It realized that it was not Azhakan but someone else behind it. Maanikkan turned to the left with a snort, and Chothi's rod broke into several pieces.

Maanikkan snapped the rope that tied the yoke, attacked Maniyan and then turned towards Chothi. In panic the on-lookers fled the banks. Chothi too was a fast runner. But unfortunately, he slipped on a narrow embankment and fell headlong into the field. Oh, no! Thousand voices cried out in horror. Maanikkan almost reached Chothi ...

Azhakan was laughing all the while seeing Chothi run. Now, he rushed towards Maanikkan. But the bull was in no mood to listen to Azhakan's pleas and orders. It wanted to tear its enemy to pieces. It bent towards Chothi and Azhakan froze. He didn't know what came over him. He pulled the bull, which looked as fierce as the god of death, by its ears and thrashed it once with all his might. Its back was ripped. Azhakan put a knot around it with a small piece of rope and took it to his hut. Blood flowed from its wound soiling the silky hair. What would the master say? Neeli started crying. Karumban scolded him. Azhakan too was remorseful. He never thought the lash would turn this severe. A fellow being's life was in danger and he forgot everything else. There was only an inch of space between Maanikkan's horns and Chothi's back. But coming to think of that, what did this mute animal do? Who had hurt it first? It was only heroic to fight back. Maanikkan was a bull. Should it not have any dignity and valour?

Azhakan rubbed *neem* oil into its wound. He gave it his share of gruel and tapioca. He didn't eat that day. Neither did he sleep. He was sorry and exhausted, and he began running a fever by dawn. His body ached and he was shivering. But what would the master think if he didn't turn up for work the next morning?

His *pulaya*[2] neighbours told him that the master flew into a rage when he got to know about Azhakan whipping Maanikkan. The master's anger was reasonable. He did not sell it despite an offer of Rs 550. He entrusted such a bull with someone not worth half an anna and the bull was handled carelessly, with even its back ripped open.

Chothi added colour to the story:

"Oh my beloved *thampran*[3]! It's all that Azhakan's arrogance. He did some black magic on the bull so that no one else could touch it. I have heard him making promises of offerings to Karimala Chathavu many times."

The master too felt that this could be the reason for no one turning up with a suitable price for Maanikkan. His doubts were strengthened when Azhakan did not turn up for work for two days. "Drag that haughty slave by the ear and bring him to me. Get that bull also." The master's order favoured Chothi. Azhakan was shivering with fever when Chothi reached his hut. He shouted in a vengeful voice:

---

2 a dalit subcaste

3 lord

"Get up, Azhakan! The master has ordered to bring you to him on your Maanikkan's back."

Azhakan didn't say anything. He knew this was not the time to speak. He helplessly watched an outsider taking Maanikkan away. Neeli cried. The bull bellowed. Azhakan lowered his head and lay down with a broken heart. He would never again see Maanikkan's head at the door. He would never hear its bell jingle anymore. The sound of its hoofs was fading away.

But what was that commotion in the by-lane? Was Maanikkan running away from their grasp? It was tethered with two pieces of rope and a nose string. But that wasn't enough to stop Maanikkan. Shaking its head it ran with a snort. One person was hurled away, another fled for his life. Only the brave Chothi didn't loosen his grip. At the end of the curved path, the bull took him in its horns and flung him away. He fell down hitting a tree's branch and broke his leg.

Maanikkan ran wild like a mad elephant, ruining a hut, some fences and destroying many crops. People screamed in fear.

Hearing the clamour, Azhakan came out of the hut leaning on a stick for support. That very moment Maanikkan returned peacefully. As usual it went and stood near Azhakan rubbing itself against him as if nothing had happened, and then walked back to its bed of hay.

Tears of joy and sorrow welled up in Azhakan's eyes. He

kissed it hugging its thick chin. The same Maanikkan who had been running around like a murderous elephant stood in his cuddle, docile like a deer. Azhakan wept with unrestrained anguish:

"It's our fate, dear. Otherwise, why should you run like that the other day, and the master feel this way? I don't know what is going to happen now!"

He knew this reunion was momentary. His master had a fierce temper and his punishment was very severe. His order would crack even a rock. How did a Pulaya youth and his bull matter to him!

Azhakan knew for sure who it was when he saw a shadow in the doorway. Behind him were 10-20 wrestlers, with ropes, rods and chains. 'What was this for?' Azhakan felt like fainting. He could bear the harsh words of his master, but not the sword of lightning from those eyes. Utterly desperate, he hid his head on Maanikkan's back with dread. A blow came down on their heads as if the sky had bowed down ... Then everything grew faint.

Many days passed. When Azhakan opened his eyes, Neeli was at his side, crying. She was rubbing oil into the wounds in his hands and legs. His head had a big knot around it. He couldn't move with pain. Neeli burst into tears when she saw Azhakan's drained face. All that she wanted was to see her brother open his eyes once. With the roots and leaves of all the medicinal herbs she knew she made him medicines, and even turned to black magic.

Sobbing, she told him: "Brother, they took away our Maanikkan, broke one of its horns. They didn't feed it for days and when it got skinny they sold it to some carter, for Rs 15."

Azhakan sighed deeply. He said:

"You just wait! Someday I'll get a calf like it. Only then will I find peace ... I swear upon you ..."

But who knew what the future held for them! He would dream in his sick bed ... a calf like Maanikkan. He would name it the same and buy it a similar bell ...

Suddenly he woke up from his reverie. Would there be another bull like Maanikkan? Even if there were one, how would he get it? He did't have even half an anna. The sickness cost him his only wealth, his health. Rs 15! Even Maanikkan's lifeblood was worth more than that ...

The wheel of time turned many times. In its swift turn many footprints were erased and a few new got etched. Some important events became history, some lines and shades faded out and disappeared from the face of earth. Some towns turned barren, and some desert must have started booming with human settlement. The emotions and beliefs of mankind's consciousness must have changed. There are times when it's possible to carry out complete changes like turning darkness to light and light to darkness. All these matter to us. But what would anyone know about the changing events in a poor

Pulaya's life in some distant land? Forest trees and wild grass too grow and wither. Wild streams run and dry up. These were but laws of nature.

After he married off Neeli, Azhakan felt the need of a woman in his life, someone to make gruel for him.

During their honeymoon, he would talk to *Pulayi*[4] about Maanikkan's colour, ardour, likes and dislikes. Thus she too knew all about Maanikkan.

His wish to buy a calf like Maanikkan could never be fulfilled. But the merciful Almighty gave him three dark little kids in three years. He was in complete debt and all his farming utensils were pawned. Desperate, he decided to seek work in the Eastern estates, because he was determined not to work for his old master again. And there was no one to hire him in and around the village.

Kurumba, his wife was always ill. She had consistent cough after she fell down with a load on her head in a Southern estate. Now, she was asthmatic. His elder son Neelambi was as if born with eczema. Kochukuttathi too was not quite well. Azhakan was the sole support for five lives.

He got 10 *anna* wages for a six to six working day. Two *annas* were cut at the source and he spent up to four and a half *annas*. The last Sunday of every month he went home with all his month's savings. Kurumba would be waiting for him with

---

4 the feminine gender of *pulaya*

a lighted hearth. That was the only time they had a full meal.

Sometimes Azhakan wondered: It would be better not to go home for 2-3 months. Let them carry on somehow, working in the farm or elsewhere. Then, the next Onam, he would have enough money to buy a skirt for Kochukuttathi. He was nurturing this wish for quite sometime now ... and a small *mundu* for Neelambi. He would need just four *annas* for this. He owed some money to the village physician for treating Kurumba. For her last delivery he pawned his plough with the neighbour for some rice. Now she was into her ninth month again. Azhakan prayed aloud in distress: "Good God! Please don't give me in bountiful without showing me a way to feed all these mouths."

It was the last day of summer. The sun had slipped down and disappeared from the top of the Western hill. All around there was pitch darkness and the place looked totally abandoned. Some night birds flew into the branches of wild trees. He could hear the parched intermittent wail of forest brooks running among the bamboo clusters. The forest path coiled along the steep climbs and abrupt curves like a short cut between life and death. No one went that way except the helpless workers of the Eastern estates. A bullock cart without roof would trail this path once a week with provisions for the estate. Once the Estate owner tried traveling that way in his car to the surprise of the forest dwellers. The car was returned in pieces in the same bullock cart. Azhakan had also heard stories about groups of daring dacoits who roamed around looting forest products. What all happened in the dangerous midst of the forest, that too in the thick of the night!

When he started from the estate, Azhakan thought that he would reach the village path by evening as he always did. How wonderful it would be, if all thoughts could be realized! He never thought he would fall asleep when he sat down to rest at the root of a big tree. But the many days of fever, combined with hunger and fatigue, proved to be a good tranquillizer. It couldn't even be termed sleep. A state of languor, when eyelids closed on their own, and limbs got loosened unconsciously. In the midst of the deep forest he lay like a cast off corpse.

Azhakan came to his senses when a twig fell on his forehead in the strong fluttering of some night bird's wings. Five-six stars shone above the leafless branches pointing to him the horrifying landscape. An owl hooted in a branch above his head. Reptiles crawled up his numb legs. Azhakan shuddered. Should he spend the whole night here like this, or ...?

In the distance, branches broke. He could hear movements over shed leaves. Some indistinct murmurs ... it must be wild beasts seeking prey. A tiger could very well pounce on him any moment. Azhakan walked, no ran, with frozen senses ... He didn't know what distance he had covered, where he had reached. He knew no strain in that endless journey.

He had heard about ghosts leading travelers astray. They took away men to some distant place misguiding them. It seemed the mountain gods loved human blood. Azhakan promised offerings to all the gods of his tribe he could remember.

After a steep climb he reached a sharp slope. In the far end of that curved path there was a huge rock jutting out into the path and opposite to it was a deep pit. The very name of the place, 'Pulipparamukku' sent shivers down the travelers' spine. Even in broad daylight people were scared to cross that path. Above, along the mountain ridges stood huge rocks. And below, just beside the narrow thread-like footpath was a bottomless pit where bamboo and cane creepers lay entwined. He had heard some scary stories about this place. There was a cave called 'pulimada' behind the rocks where wild beasts hid and feasted on their prey. Once a truck with its load of honey and grains hit a root and toppled down into the expanse of canes. Nothing more was heard of that truck and the driver. A dacoit was killed in an encounter with the police in that very same spot many years ago. His ghost would appear every night, knife in hand, shouting a war cry. One night a worker happened to pass that way and the poor soul died in delirium, horrified to see the apparition.

Azhakan remembered these stories one after another. Strange suspicions rose in his mind, wasn't that a flame that flickered at the end of the curving path? It was crawling forward with a groan. He had heard of ghosts with fire in their mouth ... in the mid hours of the night they would flame up fuming ...

whoever came across their path then ...

"My dear God, my Kurumba, my Kochukuttathi ..."

A shiver ran up Azhakan's spine. He stood rooted to the spot. Tik, tik,tik ... he could hear his own heartbeats. The ball of fire and the growl came nearer. The next moment the *maadan's*[5] iron rod would fall on his head and thus, another *maadan* would be created ...

Azhakan stood motionless committing himself to his fate.

He heard a shattering sound of metal hitting on hard rock. With that arose a shriek of pain. Azhakan didn't move. This was the ploy of the ghosts. They used all these devices to trap human beings.

But why was this heart rending wail going on and on? That scream hadn't come from him. It was not an uncanny sound either. He knew that a ghost could only hoot, not cry.

The bright half moon after the New Moon rose in the sky. A little moonlight seeped in through the thick canopy of leaves. Azhakan realized it was not an illusion, but something real. There was a cart that had both its sides and seat trampled and beneath it two living beings were getting crushed to death. There was a bull with its nose down and forelimbs broken and under its stomach a man throbbing with pain. One moment ... one slight movement, if that bull moved a bit, if that cart slipped a little, everything

---

5 an evil spirit, believed to roam around in the night and kill people with his rod. The victim then is supposed to turn into a *maadan* too

would go into that boundless abyss ...

Azhakan didn't have time to hesitate. He ran forward. Crawling under the cart he raised the hind part of the bull with great difficulty and dragged out the man.

"Don't worry, master! I am not the police or anything."

It was difficult to save the bull. First he had to untie and remove the broken cart. He took the wooden slabs and threw them one by one into the pit. Then putting his hands around its neck he drew back that animal with all his might. It was dragged back from the mouth of the pit. The bull had one of its horns broken ... its colour was a light brown ... its hair had fallen off in many places. In the faint light of dawn a white mark became visible under its neck. Azhakan was stunned. "Maanikkan!"

Azhakan asked with hope and doubt: "Master, where did you buy this bull from?"

"Oh," he said. "I had bought it from a farmer five – six years back for Rs 15. Then, it would work in the dark, pull any heavy load. Poor Maanikkan, now it is only fit to be slaughtered."

Azhakan was shocked again. His Maanikkan was to be slaughtered. It had grown old, lost its strength and splendor, broken its other horn and one of its legs too. Still there wouldn't be another bull like Maanikkan.

He asked: "Master, would you give me this bull? I'd give the price for its meat."

They argued a bit and at last, Azhakan bought that old bull for Rs 5, of which he had only Rs 4.50. He rubbed and straightened its broken leg. He wiped away blood from its wounds.

"Now, you can walk with a little help, can't you dear?"

The bull raised its head and looked at him bewildered.

The next morning, a very pregnant Kurumba was sitting in the verandah pestered by the hungry kids. They did not have anything to eat for the last four – five days. Azhakan came in, and with him a limping Maanikkan.

"Appan ... appan ..." Kochukuttathi ran up to him and hugged him. "Eh ... Appa, haven't you got me the new skirt today also?"

The youngest son came with an outstretched hand. "Toffee ... banana ... toffee ..."

Neelambi complained through tears: "Appa, ammachi didn't give us food yesterday ..."

In the courtyard, water boiled in a pot. Azhakan turned back in anguish and as if came over by some old memory, said:

"Kochukuttathi, you fetch a little water for it. Neelambi, you get some grass for it."

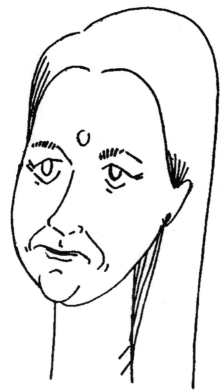

People's Court

Janakeeyakodathi

By Chandramathi

Mable Simon, stand up in attention. Keep your hands down close to your body, lift your chin, look straight and don't let your mind stray. Now, listen carefully.

Mable Simon, at the outset let us remind you that we expect from you true and sincere answers to our questions. Truth is not a mere expectation, but an absolute necessity. If we feel there is any untruth in your answers we will be forced to take action against our wishes. We hope you will take this warning in all its seriousness and co-operate with us. Having said this, let us get to the matter.

Mable Simon, what is your real name?

Mable Saira Simon.

Was this your name when you were born?

How would I have a name when I was born?

We would like to remind you what we had told you earlier. We can reach a fair and impartial decision only if you co-operate by giving us true and sincere answers.

Somebody had named me Mable Saira after I was born. I understand that Mable was my grandmother's and Saira was my father's grandmother's names. Simon is my father. He burns frankincense and tolls the bell in the parish church.

You don't have to help us by furnishing more details than asked for. Were you ever known as Salomi?

Yes.

When? How?

I use the name Salomi when I write occasionally. Do you have any particular reason to accept the name of Salomi who got St. John, the Baptist's head severed?

No, nothing specific.

In some records your name is Mable Joseph. What do you have to say about that?

Joseph is the man I married.

These words demand special attention. Do you understand that when you say you married Joseph, it means you took the initiative – either through a love marriage or otherwise – to marry Joseph?

I didn't mean that.

Then what does Mable Simon mean?

I only meant that Joseph was the groom, Peter Simon found for his daughter from a family of equal standing.

Then how far is it true when you say you married him?

It is as true as saying he married me.

Though we don't intend to scrutinize your words, we understand that your character is reflected in what you say. Now, let us get to the matter again. Mable Simon, do you know that essentially you are a woman? Do you agree? Do you understand?

I know. I agree. I understand.

Do you regret being born a woman?

No.

Why?

I didn't follow the question.

The question should be seen in the light of the general impression created by the words and deeds of women, their stories, poems and essays – that all women regret being born as women.

I don't believe in Freud's thesis.

Mable Simon, we know that no one except aspiring writers believe in that bearded friend from Vienna. We who consider starting sex education from kindergarten onwards do not require his theories. This question has nothing to do with Freud, and let us warn you not to confuse us giving answers that do not correspond to the questions. We would also like to bring to your notice that we are aware of Freud and of Fromme too.

It is Freud's theory that a woman is incomplete. And that is the relation between the question and my answer.

We set that answer aside as we need to reflect on it to understand that. Let us record just this that Mable Simon does not regret being born a woman. Now, let us get back to the issue. Do you believe in your religion?

I believe in all religious philosophies.

Mable Simon, will you refute us if we say that you are a non-believer and you do not follow the tenets of your religion?

Yes, I refute that.

Why?

Because, that is not true, I don't miss my prayers. I believe that with each prayer I purge my mind.

Then why don't you, a believer, do your duties?

I don't agree with you.

Your husband, Michael Joseph alias Babu thinks so. Then it is up to Babu's to prove that.

I am Michael Joseph. I am married to Mable Saira, the daughter of the Parish acolyte. We have a son named Tony Peter Joseph. I had felt from the very beginning that Mable was a woman with strange traits. She wouldn't notice milk spilling over the burning stove if she had a book in her hand. On the first night of our marriage, she waited for me in the bridal chamber reading a book. She has her opinions and theories about everything under the sun.

She is least interested in any of the normal things that a woman is supposed to do. She doesn't straighten the folds of a wrinkled bedspread, she doesn't clean the cobwebs from the walls, nor does she check whether the maid has swept the dust clean under the bed. She doesn't make nor want to learn to make any of my favourite dishes. Mable has to read all the time. Worse, she has to sit and think, staring into vacant space. I have seen her scribbling sometimes, but she has never showed me anything that she writes. Some of them have been published, but I have come to know only from her colleague that she is paid for her writing. We had a fight about her buying books with that money.

I know she is good at work, but at home, she is pathetic. She can't make a proper chicken curry, a *sambar* or even a pickle for that matter. She didn't even know how to give birth to a child. Tony was taken out of her womb after an operation. He wouldn't have grown up if it weren't for my mother. I fail to understand Mable. Nowadays she puts on a philosophical air and neglects me in the night.

Babu, you had suppressed all these thoughts in your mind! Truly, I don't know why you feel so. Can you ever imagine my joy when I step into the terrace to watch the night sky after you and our little son are asleep? In that privacy, the Hunter and Pisces in the sky and the mute music of the coconut palms swaying in the moonlight wake up Salomi. Then she begins to dance, Salomi's dance – with the silver platter in her hand, hair scattered and flaming eyes. Babu, why do you price my privacy so high?

Mable Simon, stand in attention. As Michael Joseph pointed out we understand that your mind is like an elusive bird. You, who have been created from man's ribs, ought to serve him. Why did you forget that? We deliberately overlook the infuriation that we see in your face and go on to the next round. Answer these questions as they do in the last rapid-fire round in quiz programmes on TV. The maximum time you can take to answer each question is one second. Your time starts now:

One, what is the price of a cylinder of cooking gas?

Don't know.

Two, how many units have been allotted in your family's ration card?

Don't know.

Three, What is the favourite colour of Michael Joseph alias Babu?

I think it's light blue ...

Four, what is the market rate of broiler chicken?

Don't know.

Five, how many kilos of washing powder does your family use a month?

Don't know.

Six, name a poem from your son's Malayalam text.

He is in nursery. He doesn't learn Malayalam.

Seven, in which market is fish cheaper by 50 paise?

I am not sure.

Eight, what are the vegetables that are not used in *avial*?

Don't know.

Nine, name the grocer closest to your house?

Don't know.

Ten, which medicine should you use if a wasp stings your child?

Don't know.

Mable Simon, let us inform you that you have got just 1 ½ marks in this rapid-fire round. This brings out the misery caused to Michael Joseph by an irresponsible wife. Do you have anything more to say?

I ... I protest.

We consider it a meaningless statement and nothing more. What have you done to make your life as a woman meaningful?

I have got a double promotion in my job. Apart from personal gratification what use is that to your family?

My boss gave me a certificate and a cash award. With that money I bought clothes for Babu and our son.

They wouldn't have remained naked without those clothes. Do you have anything else to say?

Whatever I write is published in daily newspapers.

Anyone with some influence can get it done. The dust that gathers in the books you buy chokes your husband and son.

What other benefit is it to them?

Therefore, Mable Simon, you, wife of Michael Joseph, put down the silver platter of Salomi and live as Mable Joseph. Learn to prepare his favourite dishes of *sambar* with ladyfingers and *Kozhi mappas*. Our judgment is that, you consider your job a mere hobby and live till your death as a good mother and a good wife washing his clothes, cleaning up his house and looking after his kid.

You claimed earlier that you don't regret being born a woman. Mable Simon, let others also not regret it.

A World Without Dushyanta and Bhima

Dushyantanum Bhimanum Illatha Lokam

By P. Vatsala

It didn't take me long to recognize the old town road that I had trailed long ago. After paying the cab driver, I sat for some time in the car gazing intently at the road.

I had started off at 6 o'clock, now it was 9.30 in the morning. The taxi was hired because it was not proper to bring Madhavettan in a bus. The village folks agreed with me. I should be thankful to them. Some good neighbours and acquaintances accompanied me. They didn't rally around just because it was their need as well to get Madhavettan medical attention. To suggest that, would be ingratitude on my part. How could a woman take her mentally ill husband to the town, all alone!

They got Madhavettan examined and left saying, "Nothing to worry."

No, I was not worried, because I had realized long ago – the very day he fastened the *mangalsutra* around my neck, that my husband was sick. I was sixteen then and didn't tell anyone, because no one would have believed me.

I could have told my younger brother. But that wouldn't have helped. He was in class 9 and would have only laughed at me.

Today when I got into the taxi the laughter in his eyes had dried up.

"*Chechi*, would you be staying in the hospital?"

"Yes."

He kept quiet. I peered back through the rear window of the running car. He stood there in front of our father's tea-stall, wiping his eyes with the back of his hand and rubbing it on the trouser.

Now I was standing on the street that was mine for five years. This place couldn't be called a town now. It was a city, according to newspaper statistics, one of the biggest in the state.

But my child wouldn't cease to be mine however big he grew. To me, who didn't have a child, this was my baby. Or, was I, an older child of this city? It was all the same.

This place had changed so much! So would I have, in these fourteen years. If I came across some old acquaintances, they might wonder, "Aha, is this really Sarojini?"

I hoped to meet my friend here, Varada, my Dushyanta. This evening I would go to her house. Now, it was the time of deluge on the streets – waves surged forward from far-off. Waves of people, bees, vehicles, crows. They rippled in the western wind, lost direction, got trapped in undercurrents creating eddies. The policeman at the traffic junction moved his limbs, but his gestures failed to bring results. It was all as if in a tableau. There was no point hanging around here, everything had been sucked into the whirlpool. Let the tide subside, then, I'd gather old shells from the litter washed ashore, and with them, Varada too.

After doctor's check up and observation, now Madhavettan would be resting in bed no.2 of the second ward. One of his friends had given me a food packet and had said: 'Have it at leisure in the room. It's for the two of you.' Then, they were all gone, relieved of washing their hands off Madhevettan.

Earlier, this used to be Colonel Rajan's hospital. The name board had changed, and the building too. The only thing that remained the same was the deserted corporation park opposite the hospital, where flowerless plants grew in a row. Around it was a fence of iron bars.

'Hospital for the mentally ill', the inert words stared from the top of the large gate, that remained open. On both sides of the courtyard vehicles lay reflecting in silence. The hospital had a large clientele of patients.

Inside the gate were collapsible iron grills and a glass door leading to a narrow stairway. Scenes of town life were splattered on the transparent glass wall closely barred with iron grills on both sides. With the curiosity of a villager, I put my palms to the sides of my face and tried to see what was inside. I didn't expect a guard to sit on one of the upper steps of the stairs to the hospital.

"What are you staring at? Come in."

"Please walk fast." Somebody said. There were people going up and down the stairs. The stairway was hardly three feet wide. I climbed up quickly. A horde of people flocked the corridor. It was difficult to tell between patients and bystanders. The doors of consulting rooms were closed. Two or three doctors saw patients there.

Doctor Colonel Rajan had only one consulting room in as much space. In the old building, his consulting room faced the park. All kinds of diseases were greeted in that one room, with no discrimination against patients or body parts. A rotting infected ear, shaky tooth, breathless chest, intestine playing football with food, and uterus unwilling to conceive – they were all equally miserable. In Dr Rajan's consulting room, they got comfort, kind words and strong medicines. Sometimes, men from distant villages called on him to take him with them. Then, the doctor would carry his bag and rush with them through the streets in his World War vintage car.

The doctor's daughter was my classmate. There were times when she didn't see her father for days together. Her mother was no more. All she had was an elderly, partially blind maid.

Varada must be staying somewhere nearby. It was improbable that a family would lose all its roots in 14 years. Varada could never imagine a life away from the city. She was the only girl in my class who went cycling every day. The children in girls' schools were coy about riding a cycle. Our class teacher reminded us at times that it was all right if Varada, a doctor's daughter, did it. But if a tea-stall owner's daughter went round the town on a cycle, that could be termed arrogance. For her, there plied buses from the town to the village and back.

I took away my eyes from the chaos on the streets and went into the doctor's cabin.

"Are you Shakuntala, Madhavan's wife?"

"No. I am Sarojini."

"Did I get it wrong then? Madhavan said ..."

"But doctor, you should call me Sarojini."

"Oh! There's such a custom among some communities to change wife's name after marriage. But then, no one seeks our consent when we are named."

The doctor was laughing. I should laugh too. I wanted to tell him that it was Shakuntala who made Madhavettan sick, all because I was once Shakuntala on stage! But it was better to ask oneself, Sarojini, are you Madhavettan's Sarojini or Dushyanta's Shakuntala?

The window behind the doctor's chair had no iron bars; instead there was just an open space. I looked beyond it with hazy eyes – the school that I went to, the school where I studied for five years. It was girls' school where men were not allowed. We had a headmistress who should have been born in the last

101

century. Her face darkened when school's anniversary day celebration was mentioned. There were no such conventions. Times had changed, our brave class teacher reminded her, and it was the 100th anniversary of our school.

"Is it so?"

"Yes. We came to know of it from a newspaper report."

The headmistress's face clouded over again hearing the word, newspaper. "Is it necessary? Then these reporters would keep stepping in and out of this place."

"But they would also come to know why we aren't celebrating a centenary."

The headmistress grunted. The play, Shakuntalam was the result of it.

Varada, Dr. Rajan's well-built daughter, willingly took up the role of Dushyanta. She wanted to spend as much time as she could outside her home. Varada declared that I should be Shakuntala. Darkness spread into my eyes. Going on stage? God! Varada hugged me seeing me tremble in fear, "Why are you scared? I am with you."

"I can't memorise dialogues."

"Plays aren't mugged up."

"Then?"

"Everything will be all right when it is time."

The first rehearsal was a complete flop. Words got knotted in my throat.

"No. We don't need any more rehearsals. Just put your mind on it." Varada said.

At lunch-break, from that shop – oh, that shop wasn't there anymore. In that place was a Maruti showroom with marble walls. Inside, there were cars of different shades luring the passers by. Earlier, there used to be a building with a low ceiling here. Its outhouse had a cycle lending shop. Varada used to hire a cycle from there. She made me bold enough to sit behind her on the cycle carrier. Even then, she must have realized that I would never be able to ride a cycle in this life.

Our cycle went all the way to the beach enjoying the cuddle of sea breeze. Initially children of the fisher folk used to crowd around us, trying to fool around the cycle tyre and make it flat. Varada slapped one of them on the face and gifted her sweet smile to the rest and enticed them. Our destination was the Chavoke woods by the beach. We rested on the sands putting aside the bicycle. Dushyanta fondled me searching for the thorn that couldn't get stuck on my sandaled foot and tenderly kissed my oily smooth cheeks. Varada made me realize that theatre was life.

Our play, Shakuntalam took the stage by storm. Summer holidays started the very next day. I remained in my small village home behind the tea-stall.

One sleepy afternoon, thunder burst down on our verandah.

"*Edi*, Sarojini ..."

Was that really my father? I didn't inch from my place.

Mother moved to the front room hesitatingly.

"Here, this is for your daughter ..."

"What is this?"

"A love letter."

"Oh, my God!"

"I had warned you earlier, that she shouldn't be sent to school ..."

It was a love letter from Dushyanta.

"Who is this Dushyanta, child? Is this a false name?"

"No!"

"Why should he send you letters?"

"It's not he, it's a she ..."

My brother laughed out. I ran to him and quenched my anger on both his cheeks.

Dushyanta's letters came one after another though I never replied to any of them. Father must have feared that I would get pregnant through the letters. Madhavettan was father's assistant in the tea-stall. When the *pandal* came up in the courtyard Ammalu who milled paddy in our house muttered: "This is a bit too much ... at least they could have waited till the girl finished her school"

On the wedding night, Madhavettan shook my shoulders with his hands made rough by drawing water from the well. "Will his letters come again?" At first, I felt like breaking into tears. But no, I wouldn't when he was looking on. That would be too disgraceful.

"Don't worry. Forget about it."

"About what?"

"Letters. About Dushyanta's letters."

I hooked him on the corner of my eyes and lifted him to the skies. He got frightened.

"Dear, dear! I won't ask anything about him anymore. Is it all right?"

After some time, he asked again.

"Can I call you Shakuntala?"

"No."

"That name suits you better."

"I told you no."

And today Madhavettan had told the doctor that his wife's name was Shakuntala. I turned red with shame. Who said Madhavettan was sick? Yes, I did!

The day after our marriage, Madhavettan began to eat *paan* and redden his lips.

"How did he acquire this new habit?" father asked mother.

"Earlier, did you spare him even for a second to stand and scratch his head, let alone eat *paan*?"

Each time he had *paan*, Madhavettan asked me: "Look, aren't my lips red?"

"Um."

"A deep red?"

"See for yourself in the mirror."

One day Madhavettan told me, "Eating *paan* is the mark of valiant men. Their lips are a deep red as if they have drunk blood "

Another day, Madhavettan bought a red tooth powder from town. Brushing his teeth by the well and spewing out the red spit, Madhavettan told me:

"Now, I am Bhima. Haven't you seen Bhima scooping out Dushasana's intestines, drinking and spitting out blood? But then, have you seen any *kathakali* at all? You prefer those silly stupid plays." When I stared at him, he suddenly washed his mouth and walked to the tea-stall.

I became aware of the magnitude of the situation yesterday night. Madhavettan approached me to tie my hair with red spittle in his hands. The time had come.

"He behaves quite odd in the tea-stall too." Father told mother.

That was how I reached here. I wanted to take him to Dr Rajan's hospital. I'd do what he advised me. He was the only one doctor I knew who treated all kinds of diseases. Varada's father would help me. Also, the desire to see Varada was still alive in my heart, though I had tried to keep her out of my mind, all these years.

I should buy some snacks for Madhavettan from the hospital

canteen. Hearing my footsteps Madhavettan raised his head. His mouth without *paan* had turned pale and resembled that of some strange creature. When I took out my wallet, he asked:

"Will you buy *paan*?"

"I should ask the doctor."

"What?" A voice came from the next bed. "What disease does anyone in this ward have that bars eating *paan*?" A young man in the next bed was enjoying a film magazine. He looked at the pictures with delight, holding the magazine upside down. "Sister, will you get me two toffees, please?" he pleaded.

"Yes." I said.

"Don't forget to buy the tooth powder." Madhavettan reminded me.

I heard Madhavettan's voice as I turned my face and walked away: "Tell me Ramesa, isn't Bhima a cut above Dushyanta?" A shiver ran up my spine.

The guard smoking *beedi* at the foot of the stairs asked: "Where are you off to?"

"To buy tooth powder. And, bananas."

"Everything is available in the canteen here."

I cast away his advice and climbed down the stairs. The collapsible gate was now closed tightly; one person could hardly pass through it.

The tide on the streets hadn't receded yet and my favourite street was still completely submerged. Varada's house was beyond this street on a path that lay close to the school compound fading westwards. Would that path have turned into a big street? Would the tide of traffic have uprooted Varada's house, that huge tree, which gave me shelter? How would I cross these swelling waves? People scrambled along crushing the zebra line under their feet – an endless race between vehicles and pedestrians.

Behind me and ahead of me were people waiting impatiently to reach the other side. I braved the traffic and crossed the street with them. For a brief moment we served as guards and shields for each other, coming from somewhere and going to some unknown destinations.

Now, the road to Varada's house lay ahead of me. It looked the same, with pushcarts parked on both sides. Only the number of potholes had increased. Buildings on either side seemed like school kids, breathless and crammed to the full, yet cheerful.

At the first sight I could make out that something had happened to Varada's house. The old wooden doors and windows shining with lacquer had become like the faces of girls coming out of a beauty parlour – sallow in make up. The transparent drapes on the windows and doors exposed the naked interiors. I felt that the house had turned into a ladies hostel.

Women's garments hung on the clothesline in the backyard. Two women were taking them out and piling them on their arm. The heavily made up faces turned hearing the sound of the opening gate.

The spot where Dr Rajan's name board hung looked like a small rectangular window to the past. The board wasn't there anymore, but on the wall, the marks of nails appeared like empty sockets.

Had Varada left this place? Would she have got married, sold off the house and gone far away, leaving behind all her memories? My brooding mind couldn't imagine her in the role of a wife.

A third girl, with bright lipstick, came down the steps and smiled at me. I asked her:

"Where is Varada?"

"Who?"

"Varada, who used to live here – Dr Colonel Rajan's daughter."

"Oh, madam? She hasn't gone anywhere. She still stays here."

The girl twisted her eyebrows and scanned me from head to toe. Then, without saying another word, she moved aside the curtains and disappeared.

I missed a heartbeat seeing Varada at the door. 'Varada, Varada, here I am ... your ... Shakuntala!'

Varada came down the steps holding out both her hands. She took my face in her palms and said: "It has been a long time, my darling!"

I became restless aware of the glances closing in on us through the windows. A fire started to burn within me and my body hair became blazing flames.

Varada scooped me up and took me inside.

I sat on a sofa in Varada's room with a parched throat. My eyes burned.

She poured sherbet in a large glass with a long stem and put it to my lips.

"Drink this. You have lost weight."

I couldn't speak. She looked at my *mangalsutra* and asked:

"You were in a hurry to get married, weren't you? You didn't even get time to reply to my letters."

I kept quiet.

"Look, the dirt under your fingers. You haven't even bathed today. And, just look at your clothes!"

I scratched on the mucky cotton sari with my fingernails. She raised my chin and said with annoyance:

"Fool! I never thought you were this stupid."

I wrinkled up within my skin and turned into an insect. Varada's chubby cheeks had filled out her high cheekbones. She drew her hands through her hair cut short below the ear and said:

"Now, I'll never let you go."

A middle-aged woman came in with a tray of two cups of tea.

"Keep it there and leave ... I don't want to set my eyes on any of you today." Varada said.

The door closed behind her. The male voices and footsteps on the corridor died out.

"Varada, what do you do here?"

"Business."

She started kissing me all over. My mind, shedding its hair, sparkled like crystal.

Matrimony

Dampathyam

By Sarah Joseph

She appeared serene today. This wasn't her normal reaction when I came back loitering the whole day. But she didn't pounce on me or attack me like an aggressive mother cat baring her teeth and claws. Amazing! She didn't even confront me with an accusing glare.

When I reached home, she was grating coconut sitting on the shaky wooden coconut scraper. Her countenance didn't change even after seeing me. I cleared my throat. Her eyes moved a little, that was all. I felt embarrassed. Could it be the calm before the storm, I decided to find out myself. Near her, I squatted on the wet floor. Moisture had spread across her sari, creating designs on its border. Expecting an outburst and on my guard, I lifted the *pallu* reverently and put it on her lap. But she ignored me completely.

I moved closer, till I got the smell of sweat that rose from her moving underarms. I liked the smell of her sweat; it didn't stink. She was very clean, to tell you the truth, every part of her body was clean and fragrant. And I dreaded to compare my filthy being with the sweet pungent smell of hers that I loved so much.

On the sly, I moved my nose closer to her underarm. With a simple jerk of her hand, with the ease of shooing away a fly, she pushed away my nose. But that was all and I felt relieved.

It couldn't be the mere scraping of the coconut. She had been working non-stop for a few hours and all the sweat she had shed was flowing down like a canal along the long depression on her back. If she let me, I could lick up all the sweat. But if I did it, huh, its consequences could be terrible. She would misconstrue my compassion and sympathy, for something else.

She wore a faded green sari, which was hitched up, revealing her knees. Don't for a second think the sight wasn't stirring. She started living with me when she was 15 and now, she was 32. She had given birth to two gigantic boys too. But still, her legs, especially above her knees, were plump and sweet. On second thoughts, how could I be sure of the sweetness part? I hadn't experienced it at all. Now you might wonder what sort of a man I was. Yes it was my own fault. Well, most of it, but, not all of it. And she, what do you know of her? She is a different species altogether.

But for a few black spots, her legs were clean. And I should be blamed for even those spots of imperfection. When she had come with me, at 15, her body used to shine, her skin was devoid of scars and so smooth my fingers would slide down at every touch. And to admit that I had never seen her even on those early days – just imagine my ill luck. It wasn't her fault, but entirely mine. A giant that I was, I didn't have the guts to look straight on her face, let alone her body.

Uh! Yes, those black marks of my failure ... Our second boy had eczema (nothing surprising, he is filthier than me). She would make him sit by the well and rub the boils with herbs till his body looked like polished yam. After two weeks of such thorough scrubbing, boils appeared on her legs of honey. Though it healed fast with her meticulous medication, the marks remained like the memories that do not fade away. It was in my blood, the boy got eczema because he was a filthy man's son. If only she let me, I would have bought her some scar-removing ointment and rubbed it on her legs every day.

As if straining to look at something beyond her knee, I stole a glance at those faded scars. If only she let me ... ! Suddenly, she stopped grating the coconut and banged the shell upside down. Then ignoring me, she opened the door and walked to the wet-grinding stone crossing the verandah.

I was scared because she wasn't talking at all. She lived a tortuous life and her horrid experiences could take any shape any moment. Usually I got a tongue-lashing when I reached home late.

Sometimes, seeing her fury I felt like dying. Apart from throwing and breaking whatever came her way, if she chanced on an iron rod she would bang it on her head. I could only stand and watch, because she would never let me take it away. I could give her two tight slaps, but I was sure that all this was triggered off by my ineptness. So my hands would remain still. What she said once while breaking something still stuck on my heart like broken pieces of glass.

"It's my life that I am breaking to pieces, it's my misery, what is it to you? Why should you care?"

The symbolic suggestion of breaking misery to pieces wasn't as simple as said. You would realize this only if you went through such an act. I still put up with her because I understood what it was. My failures were enormous and my silence was that of a coward. I couldn't pacify her in any way, because we were two completely different people. I didn't have any right to stop the symbolic protests that calmed her. I would never stop her.

Blowing into the iron pipe, I fanned the embers in the hearth. Hunger was pecking in my stomach. Quietly, I raised the lids of the vessels. There was rice in one and some ash gourd slices in another shallow platter – the only edible things I could find. Drinking a mug of water I got out of the kitchen. I got furious at the boys who were fighting in the courtyard. Not just that, all the rage now rushed into my mouth. I jumped into the courtyard and dragged along one of them.

"Did mother beat you?"

"No."

"Then, did she coo to you?"

My voice rose to the roof. The boy shook with fear. The other one standing in the courtyard began to bawl. I left them there. My intention was to know her mood, but it failed miserably.

I was all ears; the sound of grinding had stopped. I could hear the vessels clattering in the kitchen and I stepped in dropping my anger. How did she feel hearing the boys scream? I peered, but her face looked like the grinding stone.

She was bending over, mixing the coconut paste with the ash gourd. The sari had slid down revealing her breasts. She wore a radiant red blouse, which I loved because of its plunging neckline. I always peeped at her bosom when she wore this. That part of hers didn't have the colour of honey, but the hue of ripe lemon and gave me pure joy. God alone knew why only her bosom had this complexion. I stood there, staring. Mercilessly, she pulled the sari over and continued with her work as if unaware of everything else. She mixed chilly to the cold insipid ash gourd and put it on the stove.

I felt annoyed, but I knew it would do no good. Compared to her aches and solitude, my anger and frustration and my unfulfilled dreams were insignificant.

I stood behind her with a deep sigh, and great love that I couldn't withhold. If she didn't like it, she would just turn around and walk away. But she washed up the dirty plates one by one and stacked them up. Then she took the kitchen rag, cleaned the slab and then washed the rag and her hands many times. The seasoning for the ash gourd curry was set ready on a plate. All this while she didn't even throw me a glance. If this continued, I decided, there would be an explosion before bedtime.

I saw her carrying a bucket of water to the bathroom. Running up to her, I snatched the bucket from her hand, though with some trepidation. At times, she would decline such help with loud protests and stomp about shaking the earth. But, the moment I touched the bucket she let it go. I didn't expect it, the bucket swayed and some water spilled over. I looked at her and laughed in embarrassment. Still, her face remained like a peeled piece of ash gourd. In fact, now I was horrified, she wasn't accusing me nor was there anger in her eyes. If nothing was the matter with her, then something had happened to me.

I wasn't sure for whom the water in the bathroom was meant for. Wandering the whole day in the hot sun made me feel sticky all over, even otherwise, my sweat stank badly. And it was not merely the stink of the sweat; an array of mysterious stenches arose from me all the time. My mouth too stank. Sometimes, when my breath came up to the nostrils I felt like vomiting. It must be from the yellow plaque under my teeth, which I had even at our marriage. Should there be any further reason why I couldn't kiss her on the lips for the last few years? I could see her become nauseous. Then I stopped kissing her altogether. (How could I blame her for getting furious about a life devoid of even a kiss?) Her lips were sweet, so sweet that you could slowly bite and chew the whole of it, like cherry treated in honey. Their shape, fragrance and sweetness could kill a man with desire. But could I talk about the sweetness with authority? She had never kissed me hard with those lips that belonged to me. I felt like smelling them like a flower, then, which part of hers didn't smell sweet?

Her shadow appeared at the bathroom door and then vanished.

"For whom have you kept this bucket of water?" I asked deliberately, but didn't get a reply. She went to the kitchen along with her shadow and I trailed her.

"The water ...?"

"Umm."

What did that mean? I went back to the bathroom, rubbed the cake of soap all over me and bathed thoroughly. Even I couldn't bare the stink of my undergarments. I smelled them once and couldn't help jerking my head. I forgot to change them because I was always in a hurry to reach somewhere. Of course, she thought it was a lie. I washed those miserable garments with soap. Getting out of the bathroom, I deliberately walked through kitchen with just a towel around my waist. I knew the humiliating exhibitionism wouldn't make any difference.

She was heating water again, which meant she had kept the water I had used for some other purpose. It was a dangerous situation and I didn't have the guts to ask myself why I married her at all if she couldn't even heat some water for me. My lame logic paled into insignificance in comparison with her distress, loneliness and losses.

I changed and stood in front of the mirror to comb my hair. I looked at myself and tried to smile. Huh, what a face!

But was I really that ugly? Folding my hands across my chest, I gazed at myself in the mirror solemnly and tried to analyze. I could see nothing to worry about. I might have many faults, but then, I was at least a very ordinary person to look at. Then what had gone wrong? My grades plummeted in comparison with hers and then, I plunged into self-pity.

I combed my hair, put some talcum powder and went out through the kitchen. She was getting ready to bathe the children. As always she had pulled her sari up above the knees. Her legs, thighs down to the feet, were like carvings. My legs were no good. My feet had taken after my mother's family and were fat and flat, and dark ... some inherited providence! At least I could have kept them neat and clean, but I never did that either. My nails were tattered and broken and stood out like stubs. I never cared to clip them short, but just walked around as if these things didn't matter at all. When she was 15 she had cried out in shock when my toenail tore into her body. That was when, for the first time, I took a knife and cut my nails. But still I felt it a boring affair.

After bathing the children, she made them stand in front of

the mirror and combed their hair. She rubbed talcum powder on her palms and then put it on their faces. The powder didn't clot in her hand and she took out just the right amount. But the powder on my face resembled that on the face of a dead body – it clung to my lips and mouth and the dampness in the hollow of my cheeks. Maybe it was my harsh log-like hands, but her hands were different.

I noticed her expression while she called out for the children to serve them rice and ash gourd curry. Her face was like a handful of plain rice. When I started out in the morning she had told me that there was nothing to eat. I had left saying I would be back soon. But I forgot all about that as I wandered from one place to another the whole day. These stupid ash gourds were lying ripe for plucking on the climber that spread out on the roof. Without uttering a word, all of us ate the food and got up.

The children, my uncouth boys slept very fast. She too got ready to go to bed, she opened and spread her hair – it had an intoxicating scent that seeped into the soul – and then tied it up in a knot. She opened the lower two buttons of the radiant red blouse, unfastened the brassiere, removed her sari, put it on the clothesline and wrapped a *mundu* with black border over the petticoat. Then, she covered her bosom with a towel that hadn't dried up fully. All this while she ignored me, especially when I sat staring at her back without batting an eyelid as she removed her sari. Finally, she rubbed her face with remains of the hair oil on her hands and she stretched. I sneaked a look at her – there was a pimple on her cheek, red and ripe.

I lay down on the cot. She usually slept with the children on the floor. I listened breathlessly to her deep sigh when she put out the light and went to bed. She didn't know that her sigh had thumped my heart. She didn't know that it was this sigh that kept me wandering all day. She didn't know the aches that I too suffered along with her.

As usual, I couldn't go to sleep. As always, the devil clawed within me. So, after a long while, I crawled to her and touched her, panting, doubtful and embarrassed.

Then came the outburst!

"Just lay off!"

I crawled back to my bed without another word. What was my crawling to her losses and the desires she suppressed? I could only rouse her not put her to sleep. Whichever way you looked at it, we couldn't be termed compatible.

Black Spots

Kakkapullikal

By Ashita

"Get up, man" Varghese said again with a disarming smile as he crushed the cigarette stub under his feet. Abu reluctantly got up stuffing the pack of cards into the waist kind of his *mundu*. The displeasure of leaving the game half way was etched in his mind like ugly lines on a clear wall. It wasn't time yet to stop the game. People hadn't started pouring with a drowsy bustle into the street from the movie hall after the night show. The groundnut vendor's lantern still flickered with hope.

No! It wasn't yet time to stop the game. It's all because of Varghese, Abu thought with frustration. The game was getting interesting and suddenly Varghese announced: "That will do for the day. There is some more work at the party office. The MLA is coming for a visit tomorrow." That very moment, Narayanan left, saying if Varghese isn't playing, it won't add up to four people. What's the fun then? Prabhakaran followed him.

"Come on", Varghese said with the same charming smile.

"We should reach the party office before the rain gets heavier." It had started to drizzle like the gloom in Abu's mind. Varghese began to talk non-stop as Abu tied a handkerchief to his head and walked along.

"The MLA will reach here at 10 o'clock sharp. He will lay the foundation stone for the hospital at 10.30. That will be followed by the inauguration of the collection of clothes for the mentally ill, at the *Mahilasamajam*. Then, there is the poetry reading session – we have invited all the usual saints and angels. Should wait and see who all turn up. Listen, our Panchayat president wanted his daughter to recite a poem in the MLA's presence. I got the job done. Why should we bother which party he belongs to? These leaders will vanish tomorrow. But I have to keep meeting the president. What do you say?"

Abu replied in monosyllables with little enthusiasm. Like every other young man in the village he too was unemployed, which partly exonerated him. He spent his mornings and evenings in the shade of the banyan tree, by the temple, teasing girls who passed by. His involvement with the party gave him respectability in the village. He was involved with the local environment preservation forum and also organized literary activities. On days when none of these happened, he looked forward to the game of cards that would go on well into the night. These joys were enough to make Abu's day a harmless joke.

The annoyance of having to abandon even the game of cards

after a long dull day, lay heavy in Abu's mind like the dark clouds that collected in the sky flashing a lightning every now and then. When Varghese said farewell and walked away, he stared after him aimlessly.

A rotten day, Abu thought grumpily. What else remained of it now? There was a by-lane ahead, at the end of which was a paddy field, and crossing it he would reach home – that was it. Dejected, Abu was about to light a cigarette standing by the lamp-post. Suddenly it started pouring and a gust of wind put out the match. Abu held his hands over his head and ran into the verandah of a closed shop. Catching his breath, he was about to light another cigarette when he heard a murmur nearby, rising intermittently and sometimes getting intermingled with the rumble of the rain and wind.

It was Seethambal – the lunatic who roamed the village. She fought with street dogs at the garbage heap and lulled to sleep the fields and the hills with her old Carnatic *keertans*. No one knew who had brought her to the village. Seethambal was like a black spot right in the middle of the village's cheek, a sin the world had rinsed its hands off, a truth washed in public. There was an anklet in one of her legs and she dragged along a piece of chain in the other. She laughed with the urchins at their cruel pranks, her cries competed with the thunderclouds, and her laughter with the lightning. Seethambal, the lunatic – she spent her days crying and laughing and crying!

Abu couldn't control his laughter. "Sshhh ..." He called out to her in jest.

Rattling her small change she continued chanting *Vishnusahasranama*.

Abu called out again. "Aye ... "

This time she responded. She lifted her face and asked in a soft anxious voice, "What's it, sir?"

He had made her answer this question many times, but just for the sheer fun of hearing her repeat it, Abu asked again in a serious tone, "What's your name? Umm?"

She stretched her legs and leaning back said in a grave voice: "Neelamegha Ghanashyamalambal."

Abu chuckled with the guffawing rain. Then he brooded again – a rotten day, and this rotten rain! Seethambal's chanting rose near him. A breeze blew past rustling the leaves. The rain changed its tune a little and started to teem down in rhythmic beats that matched the chanting of *sahasranama*. A little annoyed Abu called again, "*Aye* ..."

This time, before she could respond, the shop verandah was lighted up by a passing car's headlight. In an impulsive reaction, Abu hid behind the shade of a pillar. He himself couldn't understand his action. The car disappeared from his sight and he turned back to call out to Seethambal again. She was playing, tossing the coins up in the air.

"Sshh ..."

Seethambal didn't lift her face nor did she take away her

eyes from the coins. Spitefully, with his mind soaked in the drizzle of an unexplained vengeance, Abu lit a match, knelt before her and called again:

"Hey, woman ..."

She looked into the flame with the same anxiety and asked him:

"What's it, *ayya*?"

Abu didn't have an answer. The lit matchstick flared up like Abu's unreasonable resentment. In that flame he could see her dangling worn out nose ring and her coffee-coloured youth, half-hidden in a piece of tattered cloth with all the dust and dirt of the shop verandahs and streets. In the backdrop, the slanting drizzle and the lightening caressed her anklet and the broken chain. Abu sat looking at her, and she asked again, "What's it, *ayya*?"

Abu felt the surge of rain in her soft voice. Along with it came back another faded picture in memory: In the bus stand, she was licking up the left over food she had got hold of fighting with stray dogs. Conductor Ramadas slapped hard on her half-naked thigh and walked away gleefully mouthing aloud an abuse. And the spectators laughed out aloud with him.

Abu's mind burned with pleasure in that memory, as his fingers did in the dying flames of the matchstick. Outside, the rain was frolicking, rolling in laughter. Disgruntled thoughts swirled aimlessly like dry leaves in Abu's mind. He could hear water gushing through the narrow channels in the paddy fields.

Somewhere in the distance boomed the sound of thunder. It crashed down resoundingly on Abu's nerves.

He stretched out his hands – may be to retain a story to retell and to share a good laugh when they sit for a game of cards next time; who can fathom the urges of the human mind. He grabbed her tattered piece of cloth that resembled a cobweb. Her chanting slackened a bit, and then went wrong all together; the coins slipped from her hands and clattered away.

As the anklet and the piece of chain on her legs burst out in laughter, carefree in their innocence, and as she turned into a sorrow no one would mourn or account for, the frustration of having had to stop a game of cards prematurely lay in the dust bin of Abu's mind like a crumpled piece of paper somebody had flung away.

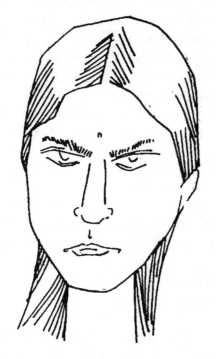

The Lost World

Parajita

By Rajalakshmi

Nirmala suddenly drew her hands back. The papers fell from his hands with a rustling sound on to the table. She picked them up silently and stood up.

"Make the changes that I have pointed out."

"Yes."

She walked out. The spring door with a cloth screen at its centre closed behind her. That was very stupid of her. He must have realized there was something wrong. It was so embarrassing!

She was the mother of a seven year old. Still ... It was so shameful!

She walked to her room and sat before the microscope.

She could hear Bhaskaran humming in the other room. He must have come across something exciting. That was when he would usually hum songs. Bhaskaran was a good soul. White mice, insulin injections and Hindi songs were his life. He was very intelligent and was aware of it too. And he was young; he would make it in life.

All troubles were short-lived when you were young. Bhaskaran was around 20-22, in that phase of life when he had the courage to face all odds.

She shouldn't have behaved that way with the director. Well, that was over now. She took out a couple of bottles of mites from the incubator. If only like Bhaskaran she could immerse herself in the experiments. But how could she? She had taken up the researcher's job only after her husband left for England. She got the scholarship because Ravi knew Mr. Varghese who was on the board of directors. If she had joined this place immediately after college she too could have done something worthwhile. Instead she took it easy making a home. Now she couldn't remember anything she had learnt. But what would she have done without this job? Rajiv was in a boarding school. Ravi was in England. And she had nothing else to do.

"Mrs. Panicker, are you busy?" Thomas came in from the verandah.

"Not at all."

"Bhaskaran is singing away to glory."

"Yes. It's been quite sometime now. He seems to be in great excitement."

"He should have chosen biochemistry instead of marine biology."

"He will finish his research in no time. He has done enough

work to submit his thesis. After which he will get some good job."

"And that would be the end of it. Look at me? My professors had predicted that I would go places."

"So, what's wrong with you now?"

"Is it anything useful that I'm doing here? The stipend is better than a college teacher's salary. That's why I came here. I can afford to take it easy for another three-four years."

"Ouseph, bring it in here." Thomas called out looking at the verandah. "I had asked for coffee. Can we have it here?"

"Of course."

"Ouseph, you sent Krishnankutty and Unni Menon in here. Bhaskara, come over if you want some coffee."

"Thommichetta, my dear Thommichetta, could you please sent it here. I can't come out now." Bhaskaran called out from his room.

"Then you don't have it."

"*Ayyo*, Mrs. Panicker, please tell him to send it."

She poured the coffee into a beaker and took it to where Bhaskaran was leaning over a microscope.

"Thank you very much."

She closed the door and came out. Why disturb him with their conversation?

The three men were sitting around a table on stools they had picked up from the room.

"Mrs. Panicker you should serve."

She poured coffee into four beakers.

"Mrs. Panicker, did you show him the papers?" Thomas asked while sipping the coffee.

"Yes."

"What did he say?"

"He suggested two-three changes. Isn't there a German journal that we subscribe to? It seems some article was published in it related to this subject in '58. He asked me to refer to it."

"We should give that to him. He knows his subject."

"That's true." Unni Menon agreed.

"If he doesn't know something, it's because there isn't any use knowing it."

"The dare devil."

"Mephistopheles." Krishnankutty commented.

"Who's that?" Thomas asked

"Satan."

"He grilled Krishnankutty yesterday." Unni Menon laughed. "Thomas, did you hear that? Yesterday, the director finished off and buried away Krishnankutty's theory, evolution of Protozoa."

"It's not so." Krishnankutty flared up. "Yes, he said it was not good. And, he convinced me with reasons. But he is bad, doesn't have a heart. Satan."

"Dark, sinister ... stop it, Krishnankutty." Unni Menon

pulled his leg. "Your protozoa weren't good anyway."

"No, no, Menon, it's true." Thomas was on Krishnankutty's side. "He is wicked deep inside. He thinks about no one but himself."

"As if the rest of us work to uplift the society." Menon didn't let go.

"At least we think of our wife and children. But he doesn't have a home or a family. He is a bachelor, too much into himself."

"He should be at least 40 now?" Krishnankutty asked.

"Oh, yes. It's been 7-8 years since he joined this place."

"He doesn't look his age." Unni Menon was still on his side.

"Mrs. Panicker, have you seen his bungalow?" Thomas turned towards her.

"No."

"It's a first class structure. Complete with tennis court, swimming pool and Alsatian dogs. Very stylish."

"But he is high by the time it's sunset." Krishnankutty said.

"Mrs. Panicker won't like this sort of talk." Unni Menon wanted to put an end to their gossip.

"No, go on. Don't bother about me."

"He is a terrible guy, Mrs. Panicker. A really terrible guy."

Satan – so did he do that deliberately?

That evening she got Rajiv's letter from Bangalore with the

school's logo stamped on the envelope. 'Dear Mrs. Panicker' –
That was the superintendent's bimonthly report. Inside there
was a small note from Rajiv.

My dear Mummy,

Got your letter, thanks, I am all right. How are you? I had
a letter from father. He sent me three stamps. Have you got
stamps?

Yours affectionately,

Rajiv Panicker

There were horizontal lines drawn on the paper for him to
keep a straight line. Someone must have sat with him and
made him write the letter. Rajiv – before he was born she
thought it was a girl and had wanted to call her Chitra.

She had to somehow get him a few foreign stamps. The
director had a letter from Finland the other day. He said it was
a letter from a professor in Helsinki University. He could get
her more stamps if she asked. Often he got letters from all
over the world. Last year he had toured the whole of Europe.

Chi, again the director! She was at it again, thinking of him.

Mephistopheles, dark, sinister ... She wanted to get him
out of her mind.

A few weeks went by. She didn't ask the director for stamps.
Unni Menon's brother was in Sri Lanka. He gave her two silly
stamps, which she sent to Rajiv. Every time she stepped into
the director's room, she could see among the untidy heap of

papers, the envelope with Finland's stamp on it.

"You don't need this stamp, do you? Can I take it out and send it to my son?" She could not bring herself to ask him.

She was nervous to step into his room. It had the smell of expensive imported cigarettes. He sat there below the ceiling fan, his hair falling carelessly over his forehead. And, beyond him through the window, there was the endless roar of the sea.

When she went to meet him, she had this unnerving feeling of being away from human settlements. Once inside, she would not be at peace till she stepped out. But her work took her to his room, once or twice a day. She had to seek many clarifications. But was she merely getting her work done? She asked herself repeatedly.

Another fortnight passed amidst Bhaskaran's Hindi songs and office gossip. She was now more or less immersed in the growth and multiplication of mites and had produced five-six good slides. She went to the director with the drawings. But he insisted on seeing the slides as well.

The director followed her. Bhaskaran was not in there. The other three were in the next room. She took each slide and mounted it properly for him to see. He saw five of them. She fixed the sixth one and moved backwards, but she was late by a moment. He lowered his head into the microscope as she lifted hers.

A soft encounter!

Blood rushed to her face. She took time to raise her face.

141

He stood there rubbing his head. It hadn't hurt her. Sure, it must not have hurt him at all.

"I am sorry." He said.

Then he laughed. But there wasn't any regret in that laugh. She lowered her head again.

"Good, very good. Congratulations!" He said turning back from the sixth slide.

She didn't say anything. She felt a burning sensation on her forehead where he hit her. She could hear Thomas's voice in the verandah. He was coming to her room. No, she didn't want to see anyone now. She went out in a hurry and felt pacified climbing down a few steps. Downstairs, seeing her, Kittan stood up from his seat at the door of the aquarium. He maintained that whoever did research upstairs should come and visit the fishes down below.

She could catch her breath in the darkness of the aquarium. As usual there was a crowd inside. She inched ahead at the end of the queue. She had seen these gold fishes and sea snakes several times.

Was her forehead glistening in the darkness?

Look at this woman. She was unlike others. She had a husband and a son, but she nursed thoughts of another man.

Did her countenance give away her feelings? Where was she headed for?

The two tortoises appeared to have been fighting. Their

glass cage was splattered with blood. She walked very slowly, yet reached the exit fast. Should she take one more round? Kittan opened the door to send in another group of people. She stepped out. Now, what? Should she go back to her microscope? She couldn't. She walked down the beach. It was only 3 o'clock and still hot. A large group of college students sat in the shade of a boat, tossing nuts into their mouths. She sat next to another boat.

Long ago, she had sat here on a hot afternoon in the shade of an umbrella. Ravi was with her then.

That was when she was fighting it out at home. Ravi had sent in a note asking her to meet him. She decided the time in her reply. She was bold those days.

Her defiance paid off – she held her ground stubbornly and married Ravi. She wouldn't have been so adamant had her sister-in-law not heaped scorn on Ravi.

"His mother mills paddy at my home." She had said, when she was back after delivery. Even Ravi's grandmother was a maid in their family. Her sister-in-law said she would never allow her to marry him. That infuriated her. Who was she to favour or oppose? Her parents surely had a right to stop her. But they were no more. Her brothers and sisters-in-law had never bothered much about her. Now, why should they bother about her marriage? In fact, her decision to marry Ravi was fostered by her bitterness towards her siblings and their spouses.

Ravi used to stay in a near-by lodge. He was an acquaintance and nothing more. His proposal had come like any other – through the proper channel. If her sister-in-law had not interfered, the marriage would not have happened at all. After her sister-in-law's statement, she went into her elder brother's room and said: "You better agree to this marriage. Or, I'll elope with him." These were not the exact words, but something to that effect.

Ravi had sent the note the previous day and they had met on the beach. Though they sat next to each other in the lonely sands for two hours charting out their future Ravi didn't even touch her. And this was how she paid him back! God, what was happening to her?

Butt she never felt anything special for Ravi even when she was fighting at home to marry him. Then, it was her ego on one side, and respect and deference for him on the other. Never had she felt anything like what she was experiencing now, she felt, she couldn't look at the director in the face.

She and Ravi were married for eight years. They had a seven year-old son. And, now she was getting unsure of herself. All because a man had curly hair, big bright eyes and bushy eyebrows, because his soft moustache was attractive on his dark face, because when he smiled his pearl-like teeth showed, because he had lean long fingers and looked like having the strength of iron ...

It was not that she had been a home-bird who never mingled with men. She had played tennis with men. She had partied with them.

This was an infirmity of the middle age — the perversions of departing youth.

But she was not in her middle age yet. Departing youth, well that was not what the mirror told her. God, what an ordeal! If only she had a father, mother and a house. Of course, she could have made a house of her own in these eight years. But she was not interested. Instead she became a social butterfly. Hers priorities were different, to make hers the best among the company's family quarters. The best cushions, the most modern kitchen, she wanted them all. She wanted to be well dressed, with the most urbane manners. There were parties every evening, visits to club and games of tennis.

She wanted her son to grow up sophisticated. So she put him in an expensive boarding school. And now, when Ravi was in England, and their son in Bangalore. What was she up to ... a desperate fall indeed!

What was the use of squatting here on the beach? Ouseph would have to lock the door and go home. She walked back. Quietly, she climbed the stairs, went into the room and locked up everything and got out taking the umbrella. Only Bhaskaran saw her. He didn't have the habit of asking unnecessary questions.

The hostel was at a stone's throw from the bus stop. There was a stationery store on the way. She went into it.

"Do you have a photo stand?"

She didn't have to search for long. The moment she got into her room, even before changing, she took out the album from the suitcase. Which of the photographs should she take out? She decided on the one taken before Ravi went to England. All three of them were in it.

She took it out from the album, put it on the photo stand and kept it on top of the table, where she could see it from the bed. Yes, these were the faces she should see before she went to sleep and when she woke up. These were the men in her life.

The next day she didn't go to office, instead wrote a leave letter and sent it across.

But how many days could she not go? What was the use, anyway? Her thoughts would begin somewhere, then meander and end at the same point.

The next day she went to office. He asked her in, told her what was necessary, politely and nothing more.

Days passed by. Now, she was all ears from morning, waiting for the sound of a car stopping downstairs. Each morning brought lots of visitors to the aquarium. Still, amidst all the hustle and bustle she could recognize the sound of his car's horn. She could even make out the sound of the car door being shut.

He drove his own car. Once he reached the building, Ouseph would attend to him. There would be files and papers in the back seat. His room was in the other end of the corridor, next to the stairs and so didn't have to cross her room. But she would still know whether he had come or not from the sound of the car. Sometimes he would reach only by 11-11.30. Then, her mind would begin to wander. Once he was there, she would make some reason to go to his room.

One day he was on leave. That was when she realized how far things had gone. It was past 10.30. Then 11.30. She couldn't sit in her seat. What had happened, whom could she ask? Or had he come early, and she didn't know? She went up to his room. No. The door was locked.

Coming back, she saw Ouseph on the verandah.

"Ouseph, hasn't the director come today?"

"No, he is down with fever."

"Is it anything serious?"

"No, it's just the flu."

That day she couldn't do any work though she sat in the office till 4 o'clock. When she reached the hostel, she took the photo on the table and looked into it for a long while. Maybe she shouldn't have chosen that photo. It was taken on the day Ravi left for England. Ravi had put on weight by then, his hair had started to thin off. She should keep their wedding photo on the stand. It was after she took out the earlier photo and replaced it with their wedding day one that she realized that Rajiv was not in that picture. She took a small photo of him and kept it in a corner along with the wedding photo.

She kept it on the table and took out a letter pad.

Dear darling of my heart! What should she write?

"Here, I am attracted to another man. I can't control myself.

It's not that I am not trying. But even the mud beneath my feet is being swept away in this tide." Should she write this?

"Darling, please come back. I am dying to see you." Would that be all right? She knew Ravi wouldn't come. "Nimmi, how can you say this so casually? I'll have to spend at least Rs 2000 to reach there. Where will I get that kind of money? I can hardly manage Rajiv's fees with what I get here. Are you a little girl to write me these silly things? You don't have any balance. Keep yourself occupied, body and mind. Then you wouldn't have time for all this nonsense."

This would be the tone of Ravi's reply. Ravi had kept aside a specific time, Sunday evening, to write to his wife. No, she couldn't expect him to help her out.

Days passed by. She knew many acquaintances with extra marital affairs. Why should it only bother her? Sometimes she would justify herself.

But when her husband was all alone 20000 miles away ... If Ravi too was chasing other women, then may be it was all right, and their seven-year-old son, after six-seven years he would be an adult.

It was a Saturday.

Bhaskaran was away in Delhi as a delegate for a science conference. Thomas had gone home for lunch. The other two were in the next room. She went to the director when he was alone to clear a doubt. He answered her queries with the help of a diagram. She was standing next to him, leaning over to see the picture, with her palm pressed on the table. His left hand lay carelessly next to hers on the table. Dark lean long fingers, 'The five-headed snake,' she thought. Suddenly his hand was over her plump fair palm. Her hand opened up spontaneously. For a second her soft palm was crushed in that strong clasp. The next moment she pulled back her hand and ran out.

No one saw her climbing down the stairs. She walked through the crowd without raising her head and reached the bus stop. A bus was about to leave the stand. She got in and sat in a corner, eyes closed and head in her hands, the sea wind booming in her ears. After a while, she realized that she had missed her stop.

She went into the room, closed the door and kept on pacing up and down. When loud music rose from the next-door movie theatre she realized that the matinee show was over. She knelt down pressing the photo stand to her bosom. 'My son, you are my only solace now.'

She took the suitcase in a hurry and stuffed three-four dresses in it. The train would leave at 6.30. If she didn't leave immediately it would be too late. She had got her stipend the previous day. She locked the door and went to the matron to hand over the key.

"I am going to Bangalore. I couldn't find Ms. George. Could you please tell her? I'll miss my train if I don't hurry."

"What happened?"

"I got a letter saying that my son is not well."

A few inmates gathered around her.

"What's it? Is he seriously ill?"

My son, may you be as healthy as ever.

"No, nothing much. He has written that he wants to see me. He is alone there. Let me leave now. Or, I'll miss the train."

"Why didn't you call Mathai to carry your suitcase?"

"I didn't call."

"Mathai ..."

He came running. He had been watering the garden.

"Take the luggage and go with her to the station."

The train was ready to depart. She bought a ticket and got into the ladies compartment and chose a lonely corner to sit. The woman sitting opposite her began talking, happy to chance upon a prey. 'My son is in the boarding. I am going to see him.' That was all she should tell her.

"Is your son in the college?"

"No."

"A school going kid, will he stay alone without you? How old is he?"

"Seven."

"Seven years? My Kuttappan never used to sleep without me when he was seven."

'It's not your Kuttappan, but my Rajiv.' She wanted to tell

150

her. But she just laughed.

"Is your husband with you?"

"No."

"Are you alone?"

"Yes."

"It doesn't matter once you are used to traveling alone."

She kept silent.

"What's your husband doing?"

"He isn't here. He is in England."

"In England?"

"Yes."

"Is he working there?"

"No, he's studying."

"So you stay all alone, sending off your husband and son to various places?"

Yes. That was what she was doing. God! This woman ...

"Are you staying with your mother here?"

On the judgment day when she should answer that unkind judge, when she would have to give the final account tallying credits and debits, what would her reply be?

Another woman got in from the next station and sat beside them. The woman turned towards the new victim with her volley of questions. She was saved or was it really an escape? When that woman was asking her questions she was only thinking about the answers. But when the questions stopped, a whirlwind consumed her.

She was at peace with herself for some time when she got down at Thrissinappally to get the connecting train. It had grown dark, the place was alien and she had to wait for some time. It was necessary to remain alert with no space for unnecessary thoughts. In the train, she had to keep standing till a few people got down after two stations. There wasn't enough space to lie down, so she leaned back and nodded off when it was dawn.

When she opened her eyes, it was morning and she was feeling hungry. With the thought of her son, her only refuge, came back all the regular thoughts about food and time.

She had forgotten her toothbrush and toothpaste, so she just washed her face and managed to order two *dosas* and a cup of coffee though the waiter couldn't understand her language. She felt like speaking to someone, but no one appeared to understand Malayalam. All her fellow travelers were Kannada and Tamil women wrapped in dark coloured *chela* who left her to her thoughts.

It was noon when she reached Bangalore. With her handbag hung on the shoulder and her suitcase in hand, she got out of the train and hired an auto. When she reached the school the children had gone to the hostel for their lunch-break.

By the time she found the hostel and asked the gatekeeper to call the matron, she heard the bell.

Would Rajiv go back to school now? Wouldn't she be able to see him now?

She had to wait 15 minutes before the matron turned up. She agreed to call him from the class when she stubbornly demanded to see the child.

He came when she was beginning to loose heart waiting for him. Her darling son, he was in a pair of khaki trousers, khaki shirt, green tie and school badge. Before she could get up from the chair, he reached her holding his hand out.

"Oh Mummy, how are you?" He asked in English and stood with a smile, still stretching out his hand.

She wanted to lift him up and put him to her bosom.

"You are a brick to have come just now, mum. I would have got it from old Ghosh this period. Peter called me a lucky guy."

Is this the same baby whom she carried in her womb and nurtured in her bosom?

"Which class is this?"

"Dictation. I always go wrong."

"Speak in Malayalam, son."

"You are fined for talking vernacular here. Four *annas* from your pocket money if you are caught."

"But there's only you and me here."

"You can't be sure."

'Talk in English, Rajiv. Let that habit grow. You have to

153

learn it.' Earlier, she herself had told him.

"Who is Peter?"

"Peter Zakharia, my best friend. Head boy in our form."

The superintendent came in. According to him, these few minutes were enough for the mother and son to speak to each other.

"Can I take him with me? I shall bring him back tomorrow in time for class."

"Oh, we have a feast here tonight. But, of course, if you are particular ..."

"*Ayyo*, tonight I've asked Peter ..."

He was speaking in Malayalam.

"I'll buy you all that you get here for the feast."

"It's not that, Peter ..."

"Umm? What about Peter?"

"Peter had promised that he'd show some magic today."

"Tell him to keep it for tomorrow."

"It's moonlight feast today. You can show magic only by moonlight."

"There'll be moonlight feasts again. There's one every month."

"*Ayyo*! Peter will get upset with me. He has promised to show it after much cajoling. Now, if I come with you ..."

She remembered what he had said when she got him admitted here, '*Amma*, please take me with you. I'll join some school out there. I can't stay here alone.'

'It's for your own good, son. Be a man, son!'

She had plucked away his little hands from around her neck and walked away. Now, it was her turn to go begging.

"Or, you don't go today. Stay here tonight. Ask Mr. Austin if he would allow it."

"I am afraid that is difficult, Mrs. Panikcer. There is no room to offer you. I am very sorry." Mr. Austin was a Malayali Christian. He understood everything.

Her son didn't need her anymore. When he needed her, she wasn't there for him. Now, when she needed him ...

"I am sorry, mother. Peter will be very angry with me."

Peter, Peter Zakharia, now you're everything to my son. Whatever I should have been to him. Please take care of him. This is the plea of a desperate mother. Please take care of my son, guard him.

Would he too grow up to be a tree with weedy roots like hers?

My son, my baby!

"Shall I send for some tea?" Mr. Austin was in a hurry to say goodbye and take back the child.

"No, thanks." She stood up. "Rajiv, my son ..." She took both his hands and pressed them to her chest. There was only surprise in his face.

My son, who has inherited my eyes and brows, when you

grow up and sit in judgment, remember this moment when your mother came kneeling before you with an outstretched hand. Will you? My son, do remember!

A bell rang.

"It's time for us to play."

She let go of his hands. She went out of the room with a bent head and got into the waiting auto rickshaw.

A mother rejected by her own son! She covered her face with her sari and sobbed. After sometime, when the driver stopped the auto, she removed the *pallu* from her face. They had reached a junction. The driver got down from his seat and stood staring at her. He didn't know where she wanted to go, nor did he know her language.

"Railway station" She said. He kept on looking at her for some more time and got back to his seat.

Railway station. The door to her doom ...

About the Writers

Gita Hiranyan (1956 – 2002)

Rich in local colour and dialects, Gita Hiranyan's stories are a delight to read. Though they have women protagonists, her perception and presentation are completely original. It was an irony of fate that this promising writer who painted life in light brush strokes, cloaking all that she saw around her in light-hearted humour, was hounded by a terminal illness, cancer. Her works include *Asanghatitha* and other short story collections. The male gaze and the potent poison it contains have been treated in an absolutely different manner in **Italo Calvino in Thrissur Express**, with the author telling the story from an eve teaser's point of view.

Gracy (b1950)

Gracy is one postmodern writer whose stories surprise the reader with their sheer strength of style and substance. There are no presuppositions in her plots, her characters both women and men are equally round. Gracy's stories often present the darker side of life of stressed relationships and animal instincts. Her works include *Padiyirangippoya Parvathy, Narakavathil, Bhranthan Pookkal,* and *Randu Swapnadarshikal* (all short story collections). She received the Kerala Sahitya Akademi Akademi Award for *Randu Swapnadarshikal*. Her story, **What mother ought to know,** looks at a singular mother-daughter relationship and is told in a high-strung pitch bordering hysteria.

Sithara S (b1976)

The youngest writer in this collection of women writers is also one of the youngest published writers of Malayalam. Sithara's stories are angry, defiant and rebellious. Her stories capture the present day life of man and woman. The women in her stories are not mute and meek, they respond strongly to situations in life. Her works include *Agni and Other Stories* and *Veshapakarcha* (collections of short stories). **The Summons from God**, can be mistaken for a regressive tale of going back to religious roots, but it is the bold repudiation of imposed cultures and the woman's right to choose her husband and reject his baggage.

K. SaraswathiAmma (1919-1975)

Born into an orthodox family, when women hardly stepped out of the kitchen, SaraswathiAmma remained an exceptional writer. Her 'women-centric' stories took a strong feminist stand questioning the male authority and dominance. She was a spinster, a workingwoman who chose to live alone in a society that despite its high human development indices did not allow its women a separate space. SaraswathiAmma's was a troubled life that cut short her literary career. Her last story was written 16 years before her death. She died an unrecognized writer. **The Perfect Wife**, is a spoof on a man's hunt for the 'perfect woman'.

Madhavikutty (b1932)

Madhavikutty or Kamala Suraiyya after her conversion to Islam is undoubtedly the most prominent woman writer of Kerala and the best known outside the state. She is also a well-known poet in English. Madhavikutty's stories portray the new woman, who rebels against the traditional mores that choke her feminine urges but still yearns for love and fulfillment through man-woman relationships. She has received many awards including The Asian Poetry Prize, The Kent Award, The Kerala Sahitya Akademi Award. The bird that crashes on the glass window seeking the skies beyond and the man who crushes it under his feet are strong images of a modern woman's life that figure in **Smell of a Bird**.

BM Suhra

BM Suhra got married when she was still in her teens and soon had a family to look after. She started writing after her children grew up. Her first work was *Kinavu*, a novel. Most of her stories have her community as a backdrop. Her characters are mostly Mulsim women who suffer from inequalities and restrictions imposed by their religion. Her works include *Nilavu, Mozhi, Iruttu* (all novels), *Moyichi* (collection of short stories). **Madness** is about a housewife who decides to take a break from her daily routine, unaware of the consequences.

Lalithambika Antharjanam (1909-1987)

For long Lalithambika Antharjanam was the lone woman voice

in the male bastion of Malayalam prose. Though born into a Malayali Brahmin family, the winds of change that shook the feudal roots of Kerala society in the 1920s and 30s influenced Antharjanam to write about the plight of women of her community. Her epoch-making novel, *Agnisakshi*, won the Kendra Sahitya Akademi Award. Generations of Malayalis grew up on her stories, particularly **Maanikkan**, which was part of Malayalam text books in schools. **Maanikkan** tells the story of Kerala society in the early decades of the last century and it stands testimony to Antharjanam's acute sensitivity to casteism and social inequity.

Chandramathi (b1954)

Chandramathi is the pen name of B.Chandrika. Her characters are varied and interesting, her knowledge of other world literatures giving them a different perspective. Her stories show strong feminist tendencies but Chandramathi protests being labeled a feminist. She believes that a writer should be impartial without being burdened with political or religious ideologies. Her major works include *Reindeer* and *Devigramam* (Collections of short stories). She has won the Kerala Sahitya Akademi Award. In **People's Court**, Chandramathi shows how difficult it is for a woman to maintain a balance between family and creativity.

P Vatsala (b1938)

Though she has women as protagonists in most of her stories,

Vatsala's canvas is wider and varied. She is more concerned with life in general and it's many crises. Her recent stories show a propensity towards feminine issues as in her latest collection of stories *Dushyantanum Bhimanum Illatha Lokam*. She won the Kerala Sahitya Akademi Award for her novel *Nizhalurangunna Vazhikal*. Other major works include *Nellu*, *Vilapam* (both novels) and several collections of short stories. A world without Dushyanta and Bhima is a unique exposition of lesbian love.

Sarah Joseph (b1946)

A leading figure in Kerala's feminist literary movement, Sarah Joseph believes in the liberating force of feminism. "Women like the lower castes are oppressed and subjugated by a patriarchal order and only a conscious and collective effort would help them see a better world," she has once said. Her stories are testimonies to her belief. She declares in her stories her pride to be a woman. Yet, her stories have employed images of feminine grace and beauty. Her works include several collections of short stories and a novel, *Alahayude Penmakkal*. **Matrimony** sketches the portraits of a husband and wife, one sick with inferiority complex and the other sick of him.

Ashita (b1956)

Ashita's stories are like soft melodious music with pregnant pauses adding to their beauty. Writing, for her, is a "deep spiritual experience." Her early stories were mostly subjective and were woven around the family, but of late she has broken free from her inner self to look outside at the societal ills. Her works include *Vismayachihnangal, Apoornaviramangal, Ashitayude Kathakal* and *Mazhameghangal.* Man's infinite capacity to inflict wounds on a woman is well chronicled, but **Black Spots** is about a rape committed out of sheer boredom.

Rajalakshmi (1930-1965)

Rajalakshmi's characters are in love with life but caught in intricate predicaments of duty and devotion. Her stories have an overwhelming presence of a patriarchal figure that suffocates the lives of women. Her novel *Uchha Veyilum Narum Nilavum* came under severe criticism that her male characters resembled those in real life. Rajalakshmi couldn't daub her characters beyond recognition in brilliant colours. Yet, she couldn't quit writing, it was the very essence of her existence. She opted for the next best solution – suicide. **The Lost World** is the story of a woman who realizes her fatal mistakes in life, but is led to do more as she is caught in the ensnaring desires of life.

Glossary

Ammachi	mother
Appachan	father
Avial	a dish prepared with a variety of vegetables and coconut paste
Chechi	elder sister
Chela	the traditional seven metre long sari of Tamil women
Chettan	elder brother, or any elder man
Kunnikkuru	jequirity
Mundu	the lower garment of men of South India
Nirapara	the traditional paddy measuring vessel. The vessel full of paddy and a lighted lamp are the most auspicious symbols for Malayalees.
Onam	the harvest festival of Kerala, falling in the month of *Chingam* (August-September)
Pallu	the loose end of the sari
Pandal	a temporary shed where marriage ceremony is held
Puttu	steamed rice cake
Vaidya	one who practises ayurveda
Vishu	a major Malayalee festival on the first day of the month of *medam* (mid-April) of Malayalam calendar